ERRAND OF VENGEANCE

RIVER OF BLOOD

STAR TREK®
THE ORIGINAL SERIES

book three

ERRAND OF VENGEANCE

RIVER OF BLOOD

Kevin Ryan

**Based upon STAR TREK®
created by Gene Roddenberry**

POCKET BOOKS
New York   London   Toronto   Sydney   Singapore

This book is a work of fiction. Names, characters, places and incidents are products of the author's imagination or are used fictitiously. Any resemblance to actual events or locales or persons, living or dead, is entirely coincidental.

An *Original* Publication of POCKET BOOKS

POCKET BOOKS, a division of Simon & Schuster, Inc.
1230 Avenue of the Americas, New York, NY 10020

STAR TREK is a Registered Trademark of Paramount Pictures.

This book is published by Pocket Books, a division of Simon & Schuster, Inc., under exclusive license from Paramount Pictures.

ISBN: 0-7434-4600-3

First Pocket Books printing August 2002

10 9 8 7 6 5 4 3 2 1

POCKET and colophon are registered trademarks of Simon & Schuster, Inc.

For information regarding special discounts for bulk purchases, please contact Simon & Schuster Special Sales at 1-800-456-6798 or business@simonandschuster.com

Printed in the U.S.A.

For my Mom, who always had books in the house, and for my Dad, who took us to all the right movies.

There are many roads to Sto-Vor-Kor but only one path.

—KAHLESS THE UNFORGETTABLE

Prologue

KELL ENTERED the recreation room late. It allowed him to find a place in the back of the room, away from the others in his squad—or, rather, the survivors of his squad. He could not face their sympathy or their concern for him, which they gave freely because they could not see what he had hidden from them.

They gave it because they did not know his true face and the shame it carried.

He could not face them, not Parrish, not the others who had been on the planet, and not Chief Sam Fuller, whose own honor and courage were the match of those of any human or Klingon Kell had ever known.

Kell found his place in the back, noting that Fuller and the rest of his squadmates were right in front of the podium and the photographs of Ensign Sobel and Ensign Benitez.

For the third time in less than one month Kell stood at a memorial service. The first one had been for Ensigns Rayburn and Matthews. The captain and crew had honored them. Kell alone had known that Matthews was *betleH 'etlh,* or The Blade of the *Bat'leth.* An Infiltrator, like Kell himself, Matthews hid his true face to overcome his enemy not in open and honorable battle, but through murder and deceit.

And yet Matthews had died more honorably than Kell himself now lived.

Matthews, whose Klingon name Kell had never learned, had died believing the lies the Klingon High Command had told about the Earthers—about their cowardice, their treachery, their imperialistic desires to overrun the galaxy.

Matthews had died fighting what he had believed to be a great wrong and a great threat to the Klingon Empire.

When the Klingon surgeons first gave Kell his human face and he began this mission to live among the humans and help the Empire defeat them, Kell had held many of the same illusions, had believed many of the same lies told to him by Klingon command.

But for Kell, those illusions and lies had been burned away on the surface of the second planet of a system the Federation knew only as 1324. There, Kell and twenty other Starfleet officers had fought Orions for the lives of a small group of anti-Federation settlers who in any sane universe Starfleet would have treated like enemies. Yet, the *Enterprise* crew had held to their principles and had defeated the Orions. Those principles had cost thirteen of the security people their lives.

Those lives had been lost in honorable battle and Kell had mourned the passing of the brave warriors with the rest of the crew in two memorial services.

Now he was at another memorial service for another two officers. Ensign Sobel had died fighting the cowardly Orions who sought to destroy an entire planet of ancient Klingons who should not have existed at all but somehow did.

Luiz Benitez also fought for Gorath and his people, but he did not die in battle. He was murdered, and Kell was responsible. He died so that Kell could protect his own terrible secret, his own cowardly deception, the deception of other Infiltrators like himself and the truth about the mine on the third planet of System 7348.

That truth was perhaps the greatest shame that the Klingon people had ever known: the Klingon High Command were the masters of the Orions and their mine. Kell had spoken to a High Commander himself. That Klingon knew about the beings of Klingon blood that lived on that world. And the High Commander wanted to destroy the world anyway—all to get a few more precious crystals to fight a war with the Federation. A dishonorable war, one that should never be fought.

And yet those primitive Klingons lived because of the efforts of Captain Kirk, Ensign Benitez, and the others—humans who cared more for the lives of the Klingons on that world than the Klingon leaders did.

That Klingon High Command had brought shame to the entire Empire.

And yet the greatest shame belonged to Kell, who had made himself party to that deception.

Kahless the Unforgettable had said, "A terrible secret cannot be kept." And that great Klingon father had once fought his own brother for twelve days because his brother had lied and brought shame to his family.

Kell had murdered his human brother to keep perhaps the most terrible secret in Klingon history. The brother was not of his kind, but Benitez was of his blood. Perhaps no Klingon in the Empire would believe that was possible for a human, for an *Earther,* but it was a truth and Kell would not deny it.

Kell and Benitez had been brothers in battle, in death and in life.

And Kell had murdered him.

He could not bear to think of his brother Karel, who served honorably on a Klingon ship, or their father, who had died honorably in battle against the Federation.

When Kell shamed himself, he had brought shame to his family. His only solace was that he would likely die before he sired a son or daughter—for his shame would carry through three generations.

Captain Kirk approached the podium, and Kell had a moment to consider the human he had been sent on this mission to kill.

That was before the captain had saved Kell's own life and the lives of over one hundred thousand Klingons.

Kirk took the podium and looked solemnly at the gathered crowd. "Thank you all for coming, and greetings to those of you who are listening to this memorial service through the ship's com system," he said.

As the captain spoke about the lives of Benitez and Şobel and about the principles they lived and died to keep, Kell realized that he would never kill the captain. In fact, he would die to protect this human.

Kell knew he could not regain his honor, or erase his shame, but he would not add to it.

The transporter beam deposited Kirk, Spock, and McCoy in the center of the village. Much had changed since Kirk had stood in nearly the same spot just a few hours before. Then, most of the damage to the buildings had been from the last earthquake. Though there had been some additional damage from stray fire, the village had been mostly spared the effects of the battle that the landing party had helped the villagers fight, since the Orions had been stopped just outside the village itself.

This time, it looked as though the final battle—no, the war—had been fought right here. Not a single building was left standing, and the ruins that were there were pitted and burned by energy fire.

When Kirk had seen this place the first time, he had marveled at the utility of the village's design and the craftsmanship that went into its construction. His time with Tyree's pretechnological people had given Kirk an appreciation of the hand labor required to build and maintain a pretechnological society.

"The Orions didn't leave much," McCoy said.

"No, they didn't, Doctor," Kirk said. "Mr. Spock, are you getting any Orion life signs?"

"No, Captain," Spock said, "which confirms my findings on the ship. There are no Orions on the surface any longer."

Kirk surveyed the carnage around him and saw that that was not exactly true. There were many Orions in the area.

But all of them were dead.

They lay on the ground, their armor showing signs of energy fire. There were others who had obviously fallen to the Klingons' swords. Many of those bodies were not...intact.

There were also Klingon bodies in the area, but not as many—not nearly as many.

The Orions had misjudged the Klingons, badly. And by the looks of the battlefield, they had not had long to ponder their miscalculation.

The living Klingons were poring through the wreckage of their homes...and their lives. That was something he had seen on the second planet of System 1324, now on this planet in System 7348.

When the war with the Klingon Empire came, the same scene would be played out on world after world. And those worlds would have names. They would not be sparsely populated planets on systems that carried only numbers in Federation records.

However, in all likelihood, there would be no wreckage to go through on many of those worlds.

And no people to go through it.

The people on this world had survived, however. And a small group of them was approaching Kirk, Spock, and McCoy.

The captain recognized their leader, Gorath, who was accompanied by two Klingons he recognized and three others he did not.

Gorath motioned for the others with him to stay behind. When the Klingon reached them, Kirk held out the Universal Translator and said, "Greetings, Gorath."

"Greetings, Captain Kirk," the Klingon said. Then he took a moment to study the Universal Translator. "That tool speaks for you?" he said.

"It does. It is how we communicate with other people whose language we do not understand," Kirk replied.

"Where is the one who spoke our tongue?" Gorath said. "He lives?"

"Yes, he is back on our ship," Kirk said. "Two of our people, however, did not survive."

Gorath looked at Kirk for a moment and said, "Their deaths pain you." It was a statement, not a question. Then Gorath looked to the village and battlefield around them. "Klingons died as well, brave warriors," Gorath said. "But more green skins died today."

"Our equipment tells us that there are no more on this planet," Kirk said.

"Good. Will other green skins come, for revenge?" Gorath asked the question evenly, showing no fear, only interest.

"No, we do not think so. They are not usually motivated by revenge, only profit," Kirk said, hoping the translator could cope with the word *profit*, which might not have had an analogue in this ancient Klingon culture. "They seek out material goods, tools and things of value," he added.

"Like the rocks under our ground?" Gorath said.

"Yes," Kirk replied.

"What about their masters, the ones of our blood?" Gorath said.

"We will try to find out if they were the Orions' masters before we leave," Kirk replied.

"And their mine, the one that could have destroyed the world entire?" Gorath asked.

"We have removed the danger," Kirk said. "Before my ship has to leave, we will do everything we can to help you. Then, others of our people will come to remove the Orion equipment and close the mine permanently."

"No," Gorath said firmly. "I cannot allow you to take all of the green skins' tools."

Kirk felt both Spock and McCoy's eyes on him as he replied. "It is our way to try not to interfere with other people's ways of life. We try to limit contact with people who are not ready for space travel and terrible weapons like the ones the Orions brought here."

The Klingon shook his head. "The Orions did not care for our readiness. They came anyway and brought their weapons. Now we will keep their weapons and vehicles to defend ourselves."

"But your society—"

"Would not exist if we did not have the means to defend it. Can you tell me without doubt that the green skins will not come back for their rocks? Or that their masters will not come? Or others?"

"No, I cannot tell you that for certain," Kirk admitted.

"Would you try to take these weapons from us?" Gorath asked, again, without fear, only interest.

"No," Kirk said. "We will respect your wishes."

"We have been to the green skins' mine," Gorath said.

"There are other things there. Weapons and vehicles. Will you teach us how to use them?"

"We will help you however we can until we leave. After that, others of our kind will help you."

The Klingon was clearly pleased. "It is settled."

"For now, I have brought Dr. McCoy," Kirk said, pointing to the doctor. "To help your injured. We have tools that can help heal them."

"Starting with you," McCoy said, leaning forward and pointing to Gorath's shoulder, which was largely covered by a burn.

The doctor had his tricorder out and waved his medical scanner over the Klingon.

"Doctor," Kirk said, "is he a—"

"Klingon," McCoy said, "I'm trying to figure that out." He studied the tricorder for a moment. "I retrieved the information from the Starfleet database... here it is. Heartbeat...body temperature...redundancy in the nervous system...Jim, I didn't believe it until just now. This man is a Klingon."

"Fascinating," Spock said.

"That should keep the xenoanthropologists busy for the next ten years," Kirk said.

"I can help heal your burn," the doctor said, pointing to Gorath's shoulder, "as well as your broken arm."

Kirk was surprised. He had seen the burn, but Gorath showed no sign of other injuries.

"There are others more seriously hurt than me," Gorath said.

"I will take a look at everyone," McCoy said. Then he

turned to Kirk, who nodded. "We can treat the most serious ones on our ship."

"Show the doctor your wounded. We will speak again later," Kirk said.

Before he turned to go, Gorath asked, "What were the names of your honored dead?"

"Sobel and Benitez," Kirk replied.

"We will remember them in our songs and stories," Gorath said, nodding.

"They would be pleased," Kirk replied.

Then Gorath and the doctor headed deeper into the village. McCoy had already opened his communicator and was giving instructions to Chapel.

"Captain, the Prime Directive—" Spock began.

"Does not allow us to remove these people's only means of defending themselves against a technological attack—especially against their will. It's a bad situation, Spock, but I would say the damage is done."

"True, but Starfleet will not be pleased," Spock said.

"The fact is that even if we could somehow convince Gorath and his people to give up the equipment they...*recovered* from the Orions, we cannot guarantee them their security, particularly given the situation with the Klingons."

"Logical," Spock allowed.

Kirk's communicator beeped.

Flipping the device open, he said, "Kirk here."

"Giotto here, sir. I'm at the mine," Giotto's voice said.

"Did you find anything yet?" Kirk asked.

"Plenty, sir," Giotto replied. "The Klingons left quite a bit of evidence, equipment, computer files, the works.

I also saw signs that they planned to destroy the complex from the beginning. They obviously didn't want us to learn about their role here."

"Excellent work, Mr. Giotto. Mr. Spock and I are on our way," Kirk said.

Lieutenant West opened his eyes, saw a bright, white light, and closed them again. Determined, he tried opening them more slowly, letting his eyes adjust to the light.

He was in a white room.

No, not exactly white, he realized. Details started to resolve. There was a chair. A door. Turning his head to one side, he saw that he was in a bed.

I'm in a hospital, he realized. The steady beeping behind him now made sense. He looked up and could see the medical monitor.

He racked his brain for information that would explain why he might be in a hospital, but he could not remember anything.

Leaning forward in the bed, he felt a dull ache in his stomach.

Then a flood of images came back to him: Yeoman Hatcher walking; the admiral; a blade of some kind; the woman who was not Yeoman Hatcher holding a phaser, then firing it at her own chest.

Then it flooded back into his consciousness—all of it. She had tried to kill the admiral. West had intervened and she had killed herself.

West heard footsteps and saw a woman in a blue Starfleet medical uniform. She looked at him seriously and said, "You're awake."

He nodded.

"Do you know who you are?"

"Lieutenant Patrick West," he replied.

"Do you know where you are?" she asked.

"I'm in a hospital, most likely the one at Command headquarters," he said.

She smiled at him for the first time and said, "Good. Now, do you know what the abdominal aorta is?"

West shook his head. "No."

"Well, you almost didn't live long enough to ever learn. When you're back on your feet I suggest you look it up."

She considered him for a moment and said, "You lost a lot of blood, nearly nine liters."

"How many did I start with?" he asked.

"About that many," she said, giving him a grim smile.

Then there was another set of footsteps and West saw Admiral Justman approach the bed.

"How is he, Doctor?" Justman said.

"His abdomen will be sore for a few days, but otherwise he's fine," she replied. "I will release him later today."

"Excellent, Doctor, thank you," the admiral said.

West pushed himself into a sitting position as the doctor stepped out of the room. The effort caused his stomach to throb, but West was determined that he would not receive the admiral on his back.

"I need to thank you, Mr. West. I owe you my life," Justman said.

The comment was so unexpected that West had no response. Finally, he said, "Who was she?"

"As far as we know," the admiral said, "it was Yeoman Sarah Hatcher who tried to kill me and nearly killed you."

"It wasn't her," West said.

The admiral raised an eyebrow. "Why do you say that?"

"I spoke to her the evening before. She didn't sound like herself. In fact, since she returned from leave, she did not seem like herself."

The admiral nodded, and said, "There have been other...incidents. We are investigating the possibility of mind-control chemicals or devices."

"It wasn't mind control, Admiral. That was not Ensign Hatcher," West said. "In the other incidents, were any bodies recovered?"

"No, as a matter of fact, they were not," the admiral said. "Like Ensign Hatcher, the other assailants disintegrated themselves."

West nodded. He was not surprised. "It looked like Ensign Hatcher, and I was fooled until I noticed her legs in your office."

"Her legs?" the admiral asked.

"Yes, sir, I had noticed Ensign Hatcher's legs before, but when I saw them in your office, I saw that they looked different—thicker and more muscular. And her walk was...different."

"You had been studying Ensign Hatcher closely then," the admiral said, giving West a slight smile.

West felt an embarrassed smile form on his own lips. "Yes, and that was not her."

The admiral nodded, deep in thought for a moment.

"That changes things, and it explains some things as well," Justman said. The admiral saw the question on

West's face and continued. "You have seen the reports of the security breaches we have had lately, assassinations, assassination attempts, disappearances, compromised codes?" Justman said.

"Of course. I assumed it was all part of Klingon intelligence's preparation for war," West said.

"Yes, except Klingon intelligence has not been that good in the past. There have been some unprecedented breaches. Up until now we didn't know how they were accomplishing some of these things. But now we have to deal with the fact that they have somehow replaced people like Ensign Hatcher with—what, operatives sympathetic to their cause?"

"Why would any humans aid a Klingon invasion?" West asked.

"Another question we can't answer yet, but you have just given us a big piece. Thank you again, Lieutenant," Justman said.

But West was already focused on a thought that was rising in his mind. An answer to a question that had bothered him since the day he was hired.

"Sir," he said, "what does this have to do with why I was hired?"

"What do you mean?" the admiral said, but West could see a hint of . . . something on the man's face.

"I have asked you this before and never received a satisfactory explanation," West said. "Why *me* of all the xeno-studies people in the service, or out of it? Why a recent Academy graduate?"

Admiral Justman's face set. "Because of your father," he said, immediately dismissing West's response with a wave. "This has nothing to do with favoritism. I saw the problems we were having with security and I just wanted someone I could trust."

"Me? An open critic of Starfleet policy while I was at the Academy?" West asked.

The admiral shook off the question. "A young man's indulgence. I knew your xeno-studies work was excellent and I knew your father."

"Why would that make me any less susceptible to becoming a security breach?" West asked.

"For no good reason I can give you," Justman said frankly. "Call it a hunch, or superstition, but I wanted a qualified person I could trust. However, I can see that it was one of the best decisions I have ever made."

"Admiral, I don't think—" West began.

The admiral silenced him with a wave. "Later. When you are back on your feet, come see me in my office. There's something I want to discuss with you."

With that, the admiral headed for the door, which slid open in front of him.

As he stepped through, Justman turned around once and said, "Thank you, son. Thank you for what you have done for me."

Before West could reply, Admiral Justman was gone and the doors had closed behind him.

Chapter One

KELL RETURNED to his quarters and immediately set to work. Chief Fuller had asked him to collect Benitez's personal effects, and he placed the cargo container on the human's bed while he did so.

Though Benitez had come with many more personal effects than Kell himself had when he joined the ship, Kell could see that they would fit easily into the container.

There were a few books. The first was something called *The Starfleet Scout's Handbook,* which looked well used. Inside the front cover, in a childish scrawl, was the name Lou Benitez.

How old was Benitez when he put his name in that book? When had he first dreamed of Starfleet?

When Kell himself had been hunting *targ*s with his brother and dreaming of great victories for the Empire, had Benitez been dreaming of service on a ship like the *Enterprise?*

Kell took some satisfaction in the thought that Benitez had reached that childhood dream, while Kell had grown up to be a party to perhaps the greatest blow to the Empire's honor.

In a way, the human had won, for as Kahless said, "Better an honorable defeat than a dishonorable victory."

Benitez died with his honor and his principles intact. In the memorial Kirk had said that Benitez and Sobel died serving principles and ideals greater than themselves.

It was true.

Benitez had died living a dream forged by a child who had put his name on a book that represented something greater than himself.

He had joined the Starfleet Scouts—whatever they were—and learned Klingon to earn something called a Galactic Citizenship Merit Badge.

It was a naive, human conceit that understanding the language and ways of alien races would somehow prevent misunderstandings that might lead to wars. All too often, Kell had seen, wars were fought because peoples understood each other too well.

Benitez had died because he had understood too much. He had learned Klingon to become a better Galactic Citizen, but because he understood the language he had understood Kell's discussion with the Klingon High Commander.

He had learned that Kell was a Klingon and that there were others of his blood throughout the Federation and Starfleet, waiting to do their duty and strike blows for the Empire. They were *betleH 'etlh,* or The Blade of the *Bat'leth.* Like the edge of that honored blade they would weaken the Federation with a thousand cuts so that the Klingon fleet could strike the killing blow—as the point of a *bat'leth* would in a battle.

It was also like the pincer formation of a *targ* hunt, when the Klingons on each side of the *targ*'s path would weaken it with blows as it charged the lead hunter, who stood at the apex of the formation, waiting to strike the death blow.

There was honor in a direct battle of two warriors who each carried a *bat'leth.* There was even honor in the *targ* hunt, because the lead hunter and the charging *targ* each had a chance to defeat their opponent.

But there was no honor in the coming battle, Kell realized.

The Empire was using deceit and treachery to give itself an advantage over the Federation, all the while spinning lies about the nature of humans.

It was wrong and a stain on the honor of every Klingon. So mad was the Empire's determination to defeat the humans that it was willing to murder a planetful of Klingons to achieve that goal.

And Kell himself had murdered Benitez to keep that goal alive. It was a cowardly, honorless act, he knew now.

Kell vowed that it would be the last such act he would ever commit.

He knew he could not reclaim his honor, but he could honor his friend. He could fight to preserve the Federation that Benitez had served, that Kirk and many others still served.

Kevin Ryan

He could fight on the side of honor, even if he had no honor of his own. And as he did, he would keep the name and face of his friend Luiz Benitez in his blood.

Kell put the book into the container. Then he picked up the next. It was titled *The Flash Gordon Anthology*. Kell almost smiled at that. Benitez had given Kell the name Flash, after the human hero.

Paging through the book, Kell saw tales told in words and pictures. He put the book aside, vowing to learn about his namesake.

Next came photographs of older humans that Kell assumed were Benitez's parents. There was also a photo of a female with yellow hair that Kell thought might have been a mate or potential mate.

Kell put them all in the container along with the uniforms and civilian clothes. Finally, in the top drawer of Benitez's dresser, he found the medals and citations the human had earned in the 1324 incident.

There were other things that looked like medals there as well. At first Kell did not recognize them, but he was finally able to read the words STARFLEET SCOUTS and MERIT BADGE on the back of each one.

With that task done, Kell sat at the desk and opened the Flash Gordon book. It was hours later when the door rang and Kell said, "Come."

Kell had been expecting to see Leslie Parrish and was not looking forward to that encounter. Instead, however, he saw Dr. McCoy standing in his doorway.

"Ensign, have you got a minute?" the doctor asked.

"Yes," Kell replied.

"Then come with me to sickbay," McCoy said, leading the way.

As Kell followed, he felt a burden lifting off his shoulders. The doctor would give him a physical and immediately learn that Kell was a Klingon.

Had that happened when Kell was first posted to the *Enterprise,* he would have immediately killed the human and then as many more as he could before he was subdued.

Now he waited, the roar of his blood finally quieting as he walked to sickbay to await his fate.

Inside, Kell noted that sickbay was empty. The doctor motioned him to sit in front of his desk, and he complied.

Then McCoy opened a glass cabinet behind the desk and pulled out a bottle with a long neck. Kell recognized it immediately: Saurian brandy. The doctor poured two glasses and put one in front of Kell.

Though he had never had a physical examination conducted by a human doctor before, Kell felt certain that this was not the usual procedure.

McCoy sat across the desk and said, "Go ahead, son, have a drink."

Kell drank the brandy, which spread a pleasant warmth as it traveled down his throat.

"I thought we could have a chat," Dr. McCoy said.

"A chat?" Kell replied.

"How are things at home?" McCoy asked.

"At home?" Kell replied.

"Yes, your mother, your brother, are they well?" McCoy said.

Kell did not understand for a moment. How could the

doctor know about his family...? Then he remembered. Jon Anderson. The real Jon Anderson whose face he now wore also had a mother and a brother, his father dead for years, like Kell's own.

He decided to answer truthfully. "I assume they are well. I have not been in contact with them for some time."

"Well, it's time you made some contact. It can feel pretty isolated out here, especially when we face tough times. Staying in touch with home keeps you grounded, reminds you that there's a galaxy out there beyond the hull of this ship. Will you promise me that you will make that connection soon, consider it doctor's orders?" McCoy said.

"Yes, I...promise," Kell said.

"Good. I think it will do you some good. It seems that your friends are worried about you," McCoy said.

"Worried? I was not injured," Kell said.

"It's not your physical health that Chief Fuller and the rest of your squad are concerned about. They think you are taking the death of your partner very hard."

Kell knew he had revealed something on his face, something the doctor saw.

"It is very easy to blame yourself when these things happen," McCoy said.

Though he did not know Kell's secret, Kell decided that the doctor was both perceptive and shrewd. He would not underestimate the human. He also decided to keep his answers as truthful as he could.

"I do not feel that I did everything I could to prevent his death," Kell said, feeling relieved to speak his shame for the first time.

"You know, there is someone else who comes in here every time we lose a member of this crew and says the same thing to me. His name is Captain James T. Kirk. Let me tell you what I tell him: You are only human. Sometimes your best and the best anyone could have done has to be good enough. And sometimes we do everything right and people still die. It is not fair, but it is a fact of the life we lead."

Kell was silent. He could not risk speaking. If he did, he would tell this human the truth: that he had murdered Benitez as surely as if he had thrown him into the abyss himself. Suddenly, Kell realized that he feared exposure now only because it would prevent him from doing his new duty as he saw it, from serving the principles his friend had believed in so strongly.

"Ensign Benitez would not want you to spend the rest of your service or your life beating yourself up over his death. He would want you to accomplish what you both set out to accomplish when you first set foot on board this ship," the doctor said, taking another sip of his own drink. "And if you don't believe any of what I just told you, remember that there's another man on this ship who carries that weight on his shoulders. Let him. The captain's shoulders are big enough," McCoy said.

Then the doctor stood up. Kell finished his drink and did the same.

Putting a hand on Kell's shoulder, the doctor said, "Now write home and spend some time with your squad. That's an order."

"Yes, sir," Kell said as he stepped into the corridor.

* * *

West straightened his shoulders and stepped through the doors to the admiral's office. He felt a twinge in his stomach as he did so but tried to make sure that it did not show in his face.

The admiral was waiting by the door. He was smiling broadly and holding out his hand, which West shook.

"It is good to see you back on your feet, son," Admiral Justman said.

"Thank you, sir. I feel fine," he replied.

Justman studied him for a moment and said, "Your doctor tells me that is not very likely. Apparently, you should still be a little sore while the grafts settle in."

"Perhaps a little sore," West said as he followed the admiral to the conference table by the large window that showed the dramatic view of the San Francisco Bay and the Golden Gate Bridge.

He felt another twinge as he sat down, and this time he was sure that it showed on his face. The admiral gave him a brief look and a quick smile, but said nothing.

"Lieutenant West, there is a reason I wanted to talk to you today, besides my desire to thank you once more," the admiral said. There was a finality in his tone that put West on his guard.

"I think you have done a wonderful job here, Lieutenant, but I am closing down the project," Justman said.

For a moment, West did not respond. He had been expecting this, perhaps not so soon, but he had been expecting it.

"I'm sorry, sir. I'm sorry I couldn't offer you the solution you were looking for," West said finally.

"You have nothing to apologize for, Lieutenant. Perhaps if I had called you or someone like you sooner, we would not be where we are," Justman said.

"I don't think that is true," West said. "The Klingons have been on this course for twenty-five years, since the Battle of Donatu V."

Justman nodded, "You may be right, Lieutenant. I wish to God it were not true, but I think you are right."

Then Justman lifted up a data padd and said, "You have done Starfleet and me personally a great service. I think it's time we paid you back. On this padd is your official release from your current position, a commendation for bravery, and my authorization for your post on a starship, effective immediately," Justman said.

West started to say something, but the admiral waved him off. "I can't guarantee you the *Enterprise* as you originally requested, because of current circumstances, but you will get posted to one of the other eleven ships in the next month."

"Admiral, I don't know what to say," West said. Up until a month ago this was the only thing he had dreamed of—the chance to use his xenoanthropology studies on a real starship that regularly made first contact and managed tense or difficult situations with other races. It was his chance to make a real difference in the galaxy, to help use an understanding of other people to keep the differences between races erupting into petty conflicts and large-scale wars. He had always seen that mission as the opposite of his father's own, which seemed to him to be to wage and win wars against other races.

Now, the admiral was handing his dream to him. There was only one possible response.

"Thank you, Admiral Justman, but I cannot accept," he said.

Justman's face betrayed genuine surprise, something that West had rarely seen.

"I don't understand, Lieutenant," Justman said.

"Sir, I cannot accept a scientific post when I know the threat the galaxy now faces from the Klingons," West said. "In seven months or less, we will likely be at war, a war that it is by no means certain we will win. I cannot in good conscience satisfy my own curiosity in a scientific endeavor that may well be rendered moot by a conflict that could cause the Federation to cease to exist."

Justman's face softened and he said, "And you have done everything you could to prevent that chain of events. From this point forward, it is up to the diplomats and, if they fail, our strategic planning and defensive capabilities."

"Sir, that is exactly where I would like to make a contribution, where I think I *can* make a contribution," West said.

"What do you propose?" Justman said.

"Up until now, Starfleet Command's strategic planning has been done with an emphasis on the study of past battles and successful tactics," West said.

"I'm surprised that you would know so much about a subject that I thought you personally disapproved of. It was my understanding that you were not a fan of Starfleet's military history," Justman said.

"Sir, I have learned a lot in the time that I have been here, and I cannot deny that there are times when we are forced to fight. And if we are going to fight, we have no choice but to fight to win. To that end, I think it is time that Command had a xeno-studies department to offer direct input into strategic decision-making. Anything less than a full commitment to this sort of program would be *irresponsible in the extreme.*"

The admiral studied him for a moment, then smiled.

"Mr. West, I am forced to agree with you. My assistant outside will have my head because of all the paperwork this will cause, but I will have you reassigned to my office immediately and see that you have everything you need to start that department. In the meantime, I suggest you pack what you need. We cannot afford to be late for our meeting."

"Our meeting, Admiral?"

"I will have to brief you on the way. For now, pack what you need and meet me at the hangar in two hours," Justman said.

West shook his head, "How long will we be gone, sir?"

"Indefinitely," Justman said. "And while we're gone, we'll be making vital, life-and-death decisions with grossly insufficient information. Welcome back, Lieutenant."

Chapter Two

KIRK COULD ALMOST FEEL the *Enterprise* struggling. Shipwide, his crew was making repairs, holding systems together, making sure their ship made it to Starbase 21. There had been many times Kirk had wondered how Scotty did what he did with repairs. This was one of those times. This ship shouldn't be moving at all considering what it had been through—a direct hit with a stellar flare while inside the outer layer of a red supergiant star.

Yet the ship was somehow struggling ahead at warp speed with a dilithium chamber that should not have powered a table lamp and half a dozen systems that badly needed overhauling.

So, despite her injuries, the *Enterprise* was struggling for every light-year like a racer out of breath, but moving nonetheless.

Around Kirk on the bridge the mood was more like

that of a wake than that of an active starship command center. Uhura had her head down, her eyes focused seemingly inside her communications panel. Sulu sat at the helm, his arms resting on the panel in front of him, his usually busy fingers not moving as he let the ship almost fly on its own. He too seemed to be staring through, not at, the forward screen as the images of the stars in warp flashed past.

Kirk glanced over at his science officer. Spock had his face buried in his viewer, studying who knew what. Over the last few hours Spock had seemed, even in his unemotional appearance, to not want to talk or even meet the gaze of anyone else.

Kirk hadn't wanted to do much but sit and stare at the screen either, waiting for something to fail and the ship to drop out of warp, dreading what was coming next. It was as if he and the crew were as tired, as beat up as the *Enterprise*.

It wasn't often the crew of the *Enterprise* got like this, and at the moment Kirk knew his own mood wasn't helping them feel better. The memorial service was hard on them; such services always were, and the *Enterprise* had seen too many lost in too short a period of time.

But that wasn't all of it. Much of the mood was shaped by what Security Chief Giotto had found on the planet's surface, the overwhelming evidence that the Klingons had been behind the mining operation, which would have surely killed most if not all of the pretechnological Klingons who lived on that world.

Over one hundred thousand lives. Over one hundred thousand *Klingon* lives.

And when the *Enterprise* team had arrived to try to stop them, they had tried to expel the mine's massive warp core into the planet's crust. Had the landing party not succeeded in stopping them, the third planet of System 7348 would be nothing but a collection of space debris and everyone on its surface would have been dead.

Kirk had warned his senior officers weeks ago that war with the Klingon Empire was likely in the next year. Now they had a taste of what that war might mean.

They had learned something about the Federation's enemy.

As if to punctuate the precariousness of the ship's condition, the deck shook under his chair again.

"Captain," Uhura's voice cut through the thick silence. The urgency in her voice broke the mood and Kirk noticed that everyone turned toward her, even Spock. "We have a short-range emergency signal coming in from an approaching high-speed shuttle."

"Short-range *and* emergency?" Kirk asked, standing and stepping toward her. Why anyone would do that was a puzzle to him. An emergency signal sent only short-range made no sense at all.

Kirk glanced at Spock. Spock nodded and turned back to his scope, his fingers moving on his board as he scanned the approaching ship.

"Yes, sir," Uhura said, meeting his gaze, her hand holding her earpiece in place as she listened.

"Message?" Kirk asked.

"Coming in, sir," she said.

"Spock? What is that ship?"

"A Federation high-speed shuttle of a type recently in the experimental stage." The Vulcan looked up at Kirk. "It is on a direct intercept course and appears to be suffering no apparent malfunction or other danger."

"Sir," Uhura said, "the ship asks for immediate clearance to land in the shuttlebay."

"Nothing else?" Kirk asked. "No identifying names? Numbers?"

"No sir," Uhura said, shaking her head and looking apologetic. "Nothing."

Kirk glanced at Spock, who said nothing and kept his face its normal emotionless mask. "It *is* one of ours, right?"

"Yes," Spock said. "And it is using proper command codes."

Kirk nodded. That left no room for doubt, that was for sure.

"They are repeating their demand," Uhura said.

At this point Kirk could see no reason to deny them permission. Clearly something important was happening, or had happened, and someone was coming to tell him and didn't want to announce their presence. But he still wouldn't take any chances.

"Give them permission," Kirk said.

Uhura nodded and turned to her board.

"Mr. Spock, I want a four-man security team with highest clearance possible assembled and ready on the shuttle deck."

"Understood," Spock said, and strode for the turbolift door.

"Mr. Sulu," Kirk said, glancing at his helmsman,

"drop us out of warp and stand ready for taking on the shuttle. The moment it is on board I want to be back on course."

"Yes, sir," Sulu said.

Kirk headed for the lift door. At least they weren't sitting around licking their wounds anymore. Something big had happened somewhere, or Starfleet wouldn't have sent out a high-speed shuttle that was observing communications silence. The question was what had happened and why had they come out here to meet a limping *Enterprise?*

Back in his quarters, Kell took out his tricorder and began speaking.

"My honored brother Karel. It is your brother Kell. When I began this mission, I had believed that I might succeed and see you once again. I now know that that will never happen. I suspect it was never meant to.

"And while I realize that this message will likely never find you, I feel compelled to make the effort. I will not send it via the encrypted channels that Klingon intelligence has reserved for Infiltrators to make their report. My superiors would no doubt make sure that its contents never reached you, or any other Klingon ears.

"I wonder if they have told you that I am dead. I suspect they have. So carefully do they protect their secrets and hide their deceptions and their dishonor. As fiercely as Kahless once fought his own brother to protect the family honor, they fight to keep their lies and treachery hidden—and they have much to hide, brother.

"Though you will find this hard to believe, as I speak to you, I wear the face of a human, or an Earther as we always called them. I wear this face as *betleH 'etlh,* or The Blade of the *Bat'leth.* Surgeons altered my appearance and my superiors sent me to live among humans, to strike from the shadows and weaken them for the coming battle.

"I know now that this is not an honorable task, and yet, it is not the worst stain that I have placed on our family's honor."

Kell spoke through the afternoon. He spoke of what he had learned about humans in the time he served with them and about the worst treachery of the Klingon High Command—their willingness to sacrifice a large number of Klingons to wage a battle that should never be fought. Then he spoke of his own treachery, his betrayal of an honored friend, and his betrayal of honor and the teachings of Kahless.

When he had told his tale entire he said, "I regret, my brother, that I will not see you again, or our honored mother, but I carry your faces with me for the rest of my time in this world and I will take them to the next. Your brother, Kell."

The ship that touched down on the deck had a much sleeker look than the standard boxlike shape of starship shuttles. Just sitting there, the new shuttle looked built for speed, both in space and in atmosphere. On its side was the name *Trager.*

Mr. Spock had spread the security team out around the shuttlebay the moment the atmosphere returned, stationing them in positions to see every side of the new ship. He now stood, arms behind his back, waiting beside Kirk in front of the strange ship's door.

It took only a moment for the new engines of the experimental ship to power down with a finely tuned whine. Kirk had no doubt that Scotty was going to want to take a look at those engines before this was over. That is, if he could pull himself away from the *Enterprise*'s damaged systems.

Then with a click the door opened upward and three stairs slipped out and down to the deck. Kirk didn't know what or who to expect behind that door, but the sight of Admiral Justman startled him even so.

Justman was slightly taller than Kirk himself, his body slim but firm. His gray hair revealed his age, and it might have been easy to mistake him for a civilian if you didn't see him in uniform and did not look into his eyes. Like many high-ranking officers Kirk had met, the admiral commanded with his eyes.

Justman's blue eyes were alert to his surroundings and intense when their gaze was fixed on you.

Kirk knew Justman's record, of course. The official records of the Battle of Donatu V had fascinated Kirk as a cadet. He had often put himself in Justman's position and wondered how he would have performed.

Kirk had lost his own captain when he was a lieutenant on the *Farragut,* so he had an idea of what Justman had gone through. But Justman had seen the entire bridge crew killed and the ship damaged while facing a superior Klingon force.

The survival of that ship and the story of what followed was Starfleet legend. And now the legend was standing on the deck of the *Enterprise*.

Kirk had actually served with Justman and Fleet Captain Garth at the Battle of Axanar. He had seen those men and the other commanders do things that Kirk knew that Academy cadets would study for years to come.

But why would one of the highest-ranking admirals in all of Starfleet come out this far to meet the *Enterprise?* Kirk could feel his stomach twist. Whatever was going on, it wasn't good. Admiral Justman's presence shouted that loud and clear. And it had something to do with the Klingons, Kirk was sure.

"Permission to come aboard?" Admiral Justman asked.

"Granted, sir," Kirk said and stepped forward. "Good to see you again, Admiral."

"And you too, Captain," Justman said, shaking Kirk's hand. "I wish it were under better circumstances."

At that the admiral nodded to Spock and glanced around at the security detail still in place. Then he stepped up even closer to Kirk. "We need to speak at once. Privately."

"I understand, Admiral," Kirk said.

At that moment a young ensign moved into the door of the shuttle and down onto the shuttle deck. Admiral Justman heard him and turned around. "This is Lieutenant West," he said. "Lieutenant, Captain Kirk and his science officer, Spock."

Kirk started at the young officer. He looked very familiar and it took a moment to place it.

"Lieutenant West is here to assist me. He is a xenoanthropologist who is working on the Klingon problem."

Suddenly Kirk realized why this young lieutenant looked familiar. *West*—he saw the resemblance. "I served with your father, at the Battle of Axanar."

The young lieutenant nodded. "You did, sir."

"I don't think I would be here if it wasn't for him," Kirk said.

Something passed over the young man's face—Kirk could not tell what—and then he said, "I'm sure my father would be pleased to hear that he is remembered well."

"We can catch up later," Admiral Justman said, breaking into the conversation with a wave of the hand. "Business first."

"I understand, Admiral," Kirk said.

It took Kirk less than a minute to escort the admiral and Lieutenant West to the briefing room. Kirk poured Admiral Justman a glass of water, took one for himself, and sat, facing the admiral across the table. "The situation has deteriorated with the Klingons," Kirk said.

"You have no idea, Captain," Justman said. The admiral took a long drink of water, then set the glass down and put his full attention on Kirk. "Captain, we have had serious security breaches that have begun to seriously compromise our readiness to respond to an invasion."

"Security breaches?" Kirk asked, stunned. "Of what sort?

"Of every sort, Captain," Justman said. "The Klingons are somehow replacing Starfleet personnel with operatives who are committing murder and other acts of sabotage, of which there has been a dramatic escalation recently."

Lieutenant West leaned forward and said, "The admiral recently survived an assassination attempt by someone we thought was a yeoman but we have reason to believe was a Klingon-hired operative."

"Operative? Where would they get them?" Kirk asked.

"We do not know for sure, since the operatives do not reveal themselves until after they perform their function, and they usually disintegrate themselves. We have yet to discover a body."

"Unfortunately, there are a number of vocal groups critical of Federation and Starfleet policy, The Anti-Federation League, for one," West said.

"The Anti-Federation League is a peaceful, political organization. The worst crimes they have been guilty of are squatting on uninhabited worlds and exercising extremely poor judgment."

"Yet, the Klingons are getting help from somewhere," Justman said. "Suddenly it seems that no secret is safe. Almost before we do something the Klingons know we're going to do it. And we can't seem to put a plug in the leak. Or more likely leaks."

"Which is why you came in the way you did in the shuttle?" Kirk asked, nodding to himself.

"Exactly," Justman said. "No one at Starfleet headquarters knows I'm here. Or where we're heading. At this point, it's the only way to get anything safely done without it being known in the Klingon Empire. At first, we thought that hand-delivered code keys were the answer, but even those have been compromised."

"I'm shocked that things are that bad," Kirk said.

"Unfortunately, they are, Captain," Admiral Justman said, shaking his head. "Maybe even worse."

The admiral turned and nodded to Lieutenant West,

who handed Kirk a data padd. Kirk recognized the document on the padd's screen immediately—he had seen many similar ones recently. It was a decrypted Klingon transmission that read simply "The *targ*'s charge has begun."

"We received that shortly before our departure," Justman said.

"What does it mean?" Kirk asked, even as his instincts told him it was a very serious and very significant message.

"It is a high-level communiqué from Klingon High Command to regional commanders. We didn't know what it meant at first until Mr. West enlightened us," the admiral said, nodding to West.

"The *targ* is an animal from the Klingon homeworld," West said. "It is a pet as well as a source of food. And wild *targ*s are hunted. Apparently, when *targ*s attack, they charge and nothing except death or incapacitation can deter them from reaching the object of their charge."

"The Federation," Kirk supplied.

"Exactly," Justman said. "We think the Klingon Empire is absolutely committed now. They have recalled their ambassador and have outright refused to engage in talks of any kind. And what our sensors are seeing looks less and less like war games and more and more like a mobilization of the Klingon fleet. We thought we had more time, and we thought you had bought us some in System 7348 when you prevented them from recovering the bulk of the starship-grade dilithium they clearly need."

Justman paused for a moment before continuing. The silence in the room weighed heavily on all of them.

"And, Captain, the real problem is that we have run the simulations over and over and have come up with the same result: If they attack tomorrow, we will not be ready."

"Simulations can only show what they have been programmed to show," Kirk said. A simulation could never have predicted what Justman had accomplished at the early stages of the Battle of Donatu V.

Justman nodded. "I know that, but I don't want to bet the future of the Federation on miracles."

"What can the *Enterprise* do to help, sir?" Kirk asked after another long moment of silence.

"I'm going to set up a remote command post," Justman said. "On Starbase 43."

"Isn't that base decommissioned?" Kirk asked, shocked at even the mention of Starbase 42. The last time he'd been there it was old and falling apart, and that had been years ago. It orbited an agricultural planet of some sort with little interest to either Starfleet or the Klingons as far as Kirk knew.

"It was going to be until now," Justman said. "The place was scheduled to be turned over to the civilian population of the planet next month to be used as some science research station. Now it's going to be my new command post. And, Captain, we might very well have to begin and conduct the first actions of the war with the Klingons from right there."

"Why Starbase 42?" Kirk asked.

"All that in a minute," Admiral Justman said. "But first we need to be headed there, at best possible speed."

"Sir?" Kirk said. "The *Enterprise* took some heavy

damage. Starbase 42 may not even be equipped to handle the kind of repairs we're going to need."

"It's going to have to do," Justman said. "We don't have the time or the luxury to wait on repairs."

Kirk punched the communications panel. "Kirk to bridge."

"Go ahead, Captain," Mr. Spock said.

"Set a course for Starbase 42 at best possible speed."

"May I remind you, Captain, that Starbase 42 does not have the working capability to make repairs to a starship."

"Yes, Mr. Spock," Kirk said. "Just set course and get us there."

"Understood, Captain," Spock said, and cut the connection.

"Okay, Captain," Admiral Justman said. "The explanation."

"Wait just a moment, Admiral," Kirk said, holding up his hand and pointing at the communications unit. Kirk sat back, smiling at the puzzled frown of the admiral.

Five, Kirk thought, giving the admiral a tight smile. *Four, three, two, one. Now.*

"Scott to Captain Kirk."

As expected and right on schedule.

"Kirk here."

"Captain—"

"Yes, I know, Scotty," Kirk said, cutting off his engineer. "But we're going to have to make do with the facilities on Starbase 42. At the moment we have no choice."

"We may as well be using stone hammers for all the good that place is goin' to be."

"I know, Mr. Scott," Kirk said. "You're going to have to find a way. I want the *Enterprise* back to full capability as soon as you can get her there."

"I don't have enough rubber bands and tape to be doin' that, sir."

"There's one more thing," Kirk said. "I also need you to get us some more speed. We need to get to the starbase immediately."

"That I can do, Captain," Scotty said.

Kirk was surprised to hear it.

"If," the chief engineer said, "I can cannibalize some parts and equipment from the high-speed shuttle in the hangar bay."

Kirk shot the admiral a look. Justman nodded.

"Take whatever you need, Mr. Scott," Kirk said. "Kirk out."

"You know your crew, Captain," Justman said, smiling.

"I do," Kirk said. "And if there's anyone who can repair a starship without a decent starbase to work with, it's Montgomery Scott. He just had to make sure I heard his complaint first."

Justman laughed. "I don't blame him."

"Neither do I," Kirk said. "But he's going to push himself and his people harder than you would think possible to make it happen. So tell me why all of Mr. Scott's work is necessary."

"A number of reasons," Admiral Justman said. "First off, the planet that Starbase 42 orbits has become more than just an agricultural center."

"It's close to the Klingon border," Kirk said. "Is that part of it?"

"Very much so," Justman said. "A geological survey turned up starship-grade dilithium crystals there."

"You're kidding," Kirk said, again shocked.

"I wish I were," Justman said. "We need those crystals for the Federation's defense plans, but more importantly, they can't fall into the hands of the Klingons."

Kirk nodded, slowly starting to understand. "You think that because the Klingons lost a significant supply of their own crystals, they might try to raid the Federation mine?"

"If they discover it's there, I'm sure they will," Justman said.

"And considering the security leaks you mentioned," Kirk said.

"They are going to try, soon, we think." Justman said. "Just a few months ago this wouldn't have been a question. The knowledge of the crystals near Starbase 42 has been kept very quiet. But even the best secrets of Starfleet have been lately turning up in the Klingon Empire."

"So the *Enterprise* is going to protect the mine?" Kirk said.

"Exactly," Justman said. "And for the moment the diplomats are out of the equation. This is Starfleet's situation now."

Kirk nodded.

"Until this crisis passes and we get control of our own information again, I'm going to set up a command post on Starbase 42 with the *Enterprise* there as our only defense. In the very near future, Captain Kirk, I will have to ask you to be a soldier and not a diplomat or an explorer."

"I understand, Admiral," Kirk said. "The *Enterprise* and I will both be ready."

"If I didn't have complete faith in that fact," Justman said, smiling, "I wouldn't be here."

Chapter Three

KAREL WAS SURPRISED to see Captain Koloth when he left his room to report for bridge duty.

"Bridge Officer Karel," Koloth said, "Walk with me." And the two Klingons began heading for the bridge.

In Karel's experience, it was unheard of for a commanding officer to seek out a subordinate in his quarters. Most commanders summoned officers to them to point up the superiority of their position.

But Koloth was not most commanders. In fact, he was like no commander that Karel had ever seen. As captain, he did not waste time on games designed to keep his officers loyal to him or at least to make sure they feared him.

Koloth valued efficiency, expediency, and honor.

He was certainly nothing like the brute, Gash, who had been Karel's commanding officer in the port disruptor room—before Karel had challenged Gash's leadership and taken both the Klingon's position and his right eye in single combat. Gash had cared more about protecting his position than making certain that the weapons room was always ready to crush the Empire's enemies.

Koloth completely lacked the scheming and duplicity that Karel had found so unpleasant in former Second Officer Klak, who had made Karel one of his personal bridge guards. When Karel murdered Captain Kran and took over the ship, he had made Karel complicit in the crime.

After that moment, Karel had known it was just a matter of time before Koloth challenged Klak. As Klak's personal guard, Karel had not been able to intervene on Koloth's behalf. Yet he had been able to make sure that Klak's second guard did not assist the honorless Klingon. Thus, Koloth had beaten Klak in single and honorable combat, taking the Klingon's life and control of the ship.

Koloth had also made Karel senior bridge weapons officer, and while Karel had resisted the honor because he did not feel ready, Koloth had insisted. He had pointed out that there was no more qualified weapons officer on the ship, and Karel had been forced to agree.

"I have some news for you," Koloth said.

Karel was immediately interested. His blood began to warm with hope.

"We have a mission that will interest you," Koloth continued. "We will be taking the *D'k tahg* into Federation space."

"Will this be another mission of *stealth?*" Karel asked, making no attempt to hide his distaste. For his only mission as captain, Klak had taken the *D'k tahg* into Federation space and had spent all his time and energy running and then hiding from a Starfleet ship, the *Enterprise.*

In fact, Klak had nearly destroyed the *D'k tahg* in his efforts to run from the *Enterprise.*

The experience still made Karel shudder at Klak's cowardice. If he had not been honor-bound to protect the bloodless Klingon, he might have challenged Klak himself.

"No stealth and no hiding," Koloth said, "We have to go to a Federation starbase, overpower it, and take the dilithium crystals it is guarding."

"A starbase will be a worthy challenge for the *D'k tahg* and its crew" Karel said.

For the first time since Karel had known him, Captain Koloth seemed uncomfortable. "High Command has informed me that Klingon operatives on the station will arrange to incapacitate it before we arrive." Koloth seemed as disappointed as Karel felt.

"Yet," Koloth offered. "Perhaps the humans will surprise us before they fall. Remember, no enemy is boring," Koloth said, quoting Kahless. The captain was the only Klingon Karel had known outside of his family and a few close friends at home who knew Kahless's teachings so well.

"And there is one more thing," Koloth added. "The starbase will have a starship in drydock undergoing repairs. It is the *Enterprise.* Apparently, it survived its last encounter with the *D'k tahg.*"

That surprised Karel, because Koloth has struck the Earther ship what had seemed like a death blow.

"It will not survive its next encounter," Karel said, his blood burning for him to get to his weapons station on the bridge.

"However, High Command does not want us to destroy the ship or the starbase. We are to just take the crystals and go. They do not think the Earthers will want to go to war immediately over the incident."

Koloth must have read the outrage in Karel's face. He said, "However, I believe that those who pass up a victory invite a defeat. I will allow no victory to pass."

"The High Command?" Karel asked.

"They may lack the strength of blood to seek them, but they do not question two such great victories as the destruction of one of Starfleet's twelve prized *starships,* or one of its bases."

In that moment, Karel knew that he had found a leader he would follow all the way to the River of Blood.

"You will have your vengeance against the Earthers," Koloth said. "But do not seek revenge unless you are prepared to dig more than one grave. One for the object of your vengeance."

"And many more for those who would stand in my way," Karel said, finishing the piece of Klingon wisdom.

"Let this be our first great victory together," Koloth said as they entered the bridge.

Karel went immediately to his weapons console, relieving the junior Klingon who was there.

"Navigator, set course for Federation Starbase 42," Koloth said.

The bridge officers reacted with surprise, then grunts of pleasure.

"Course plotted," the navigator replied.

"Helm, emergency speed," Koloth said.

"Done," came the immediate reply, and Karel could feel the slight tremor in the deck as the ship diverted power for high warp acceleration.

"Many Earthers will die today," Koloth said.

Karel thought the bridge crew might shout their pleasure. If they did, he knew his voice would be the loudest.

Koloth stood, staring at the viewscreen.

He was the first captain that Karel had known who had refused to use personal guards on the bridge. It showed that Koloth welcomed worthy challenges, but Karel knew that not a single Klingon on the bridge wished to do anything else at that moment than follow their new leader into battle.

Lieutenant West used his bed like a chair in the quarters he had been assigned on the *Enterprise*. The single room was larger than he would have expected, and he had it to himself, another surprise. It showed that Captain Kirk had great respect for the admiral.

That was something that West understood.

He looked around the quarters, memorizing every detail.

Just a few weeks ago, his greatest dream had been to serve on a starship. It was an honor reserved for just over five thousand active officers spread out over twelve ships.

As a cadet, he had believed that he could use his xenoanthropology studies to promote real understanding of other races and cultures, to make the Federation stronger and safer.

He had wanted to make the kind of warfare that Starfleet had known in the past obsolete, a relic of a different age—a relic of his father's age.

But he had seen too much in too short a time to believe peace would be that easy. Now he felt he understood Klingons as well as he might ever understand them. Yet that understanding brought him no hope.

He had watched Admiral Justman work, and had worked alongside him. He had seen Starfleet's top admirals doing their best, *making vital, life-and-death decisions with little or no information.*

It was what his father had done at the Battle of Axanar and other places.

As a cadet, West had done nothing but scorn the efforts of his father and men like him. West had been convinced that had he been in their position, he would have done better, somehow avoided the conflicts that they fought at great price and won.

Lieutenant West found that he had a great deal to say to his father, things that he could never say at their last meeting, when their voices had been raised.

For the first time, West wondered if he would ever be able to say them. There was a communications blackout for nonessential communication. And darkness was falling over the Federation.

West was convinced that he might live to see its last days.

He also had a bad feeling about this mission. He and the admiral had not discussed it, but he sensed that Justman had the same feeling.

If he had been able to somehow wrangle a short visit

to a starship, he would have spent the entire time exploring every crevice of the ship. Now his mind was on perhaps the most important work he ever had done, or ever might do.

He had to use all of his training, study, and ability to find a solution to the Klingon problem. And now the problem was not how to make peace with them, but how to wage a terrible war and win it.

After the suicide assassination attempt against the admiral, West had time in the hospital and on the shuttle flight out here to think about a lot of things. He was becoming more and more convinced that only a full-scale war with the Klingons would settle anything.

And at the moment, he doubted Starfleet and the Federation would win that war. So the war had to be delayed while Starfleet got ready.

He knew he should be getting some rest, but his racing mind would not quiet.

He called up the layout of Starbase 42 on his data padd and the list of equipment still left there. It wasn't much. The place had been slowly taken apart and was about to be given away to the locals on the planet below. He had no idea how they were going to turn it into a working defense of the planet in any kind of time. But it had to be done, somehow. West knew that if anyone could do it, it was Admiral Justman and Captain Kirk.

He was supposed to be getting some rest. At least, that was what the admiral had told him to do. But at the speed West's mind was working, rest wasn't going to come easily, if at all.

West grabbed his data tapes and headed out the door.

By following the schematic on the padd he carried he was able to find the library computer room easily. It was impressive, the rival of any computer system he had ever seen—save for the one at Starfleet Command head-quarters.

He set down to work. He had spent weeks learning everything he could about the Klingons from the Starfleet cultural database, which had entries dating back to the original Vulcan database.

Now he sat down in front of one of the terminals and began a new research project. The Klingons had a long military history, and there was no shortage of entries in the military database.

He started at the beginning.

Chapter Four

WHEN KELL ENTERED the dining room, Ensign Parrish, Ensign Clark, and Ensign Jawer were eating at a table. Besides Chief Fuller, Chief Brantley, and Kell himself, they were the only survivors of the incidents on systems 1324 and 7348. They were the only survivors of a force that had originally been twenty-one officers.

Kell wondered if even the Klingon Defense Force's high-risk shock-troop units knew losses like that in such a short time.

The group's heads turned and Parrish stood up immediately. "Jon, come here," she said.

He could read the concern on her face, on all of their faces. It was wise to come, he realized, not because he needed the company, but because to continue avoiding them might cause Dr. McCoy to show further interest in his situation.

Jon nodded to them and took the only open place at the table, next to Parrish. "Have you eaten, Jon?" she asked, and Kell noticed that the others were still eating. He had to think for a moment. Though he did not feel hungry, he realized that he had not yet eaten that day.

"Have you?" she repeated.

"No," he said.

The others shared a look that Kell did not understand, and then Parrish left, only to return a few moments later with a plate of meat loaf, which she placed in front of him.

The others watched him expectantly and he realized that there was only one way to quiet their concern. He began to eat.

"Has anyone heard about why Admiral Justman is on board?" Clark asked.

"No," Jawer said. "I haven't heard anything, I mean anything except that we have rerouted to Starbase 42."

"It's still active?" Parrish asked. "I thought they shut it down?"

"I guess we'll find out when we get there," Jawer said. "It's funny, I always depended on Benitez for that kind of news."

At the mention of Benitez's name, a silence fell over the table. And suddenly he felt both the presence and the absence of Benitez and Sobel. He searched the faces of the others and saw they felt the same thing.

Both the silence and the presence remained until everyone was done eating.

Kell was the first to rise. "I must get back to my quarters," he said. For a moment he considered inventing a reason, then decided to simply forgo any further explanation. He had had enough lies; he would not begin making petty ones.

"So do I," Parrish said, and the others nodded farewell to them.

In the corridor, she said, "I wanted to speak with you."

"Yes, let's speak in my quarters," he said.

She seemed surprised by his response but did not comment on it.

Kell had known that this conversation was inevitable. He was not looking forward to it, yet he decided that he would not avoid it. Parrish deserved that much.

For a moment, before he learned the truth about the Empire's role in the Orion mining operation and before his own betrayal of Benitez, Kell had entertained the possibility of a future for himself. It would have been a future outside of the Klingon Empire and it even had included Parrish.

It was a foolish dream, he realized. And it was now impossible. He would not allow himself to get involved again with Parrish. She deserved better than an honorless deceiver who betrayed his truest friend.

She deserved…much. And he had nothing to offer her but a quick and definite end to their relationship. That was the only thing that would allow her a future of her own.

It was the only gift he could give her. And though he knew it would hurt her, he would not deny her the future.

Inside his quarters he found he did not know how to begin, and for the moment he did not wish to. He wished to simply be with her for a short time longer before he said what he had to say and she stormed away in anger.

Parrish, however, did not hesitate. She looked him directly in the eye and said, "Jon."

That was all.

Her hands were on him, and then her lips found his.

Though he remembered that there was something he needed to do, something he needed to say to her, the words began to fade from his mind like a sound that grows more and more distant. Then they were silent.

He found that he wanted her comfort, that he wanted *her*...

His blood was burning for her.

And his blood would not be denied.

The room was silent as Kirk finished going over what the admiral had told him. The air seemed thick and heavy, as if the circulators weren't working well. His senior staff and the security section chiefs seemed to be as stunned as he had felt when told that it seemed a war with the Klingons was now inevitable.

Scotty just sat, his hands on the table, shaking his head slowly back and forth, as if fighting a silent fight to resist the news.

Dr. McCoy stared at the table in front of him, his face

carrying a pained but focused expression, as if he were working on a deathly ill patient and losing.

Spock had the same expression on his face he always had. But when Kirk had declared that the war was inevitable and would be coming much sooner than they had expected, Spock had shifted slightly in his chair. That was about as much reaction as Spock ever gave to bad news.

"Captain," Security Section Chief Sam Fuller said. "Can we tell our people what we are up against?"

"Yes," Kirk said. "There is no more pretense. The war is coming and Starfleet needs to prepare. Even the diplomats think they have exhausted all avenues."

"All because a Klingon dog—"

"A *targ,* Doctor," Spock said.

"Just because we intercepted a message about a Klingon *dog,*" McCoy said.

"Bones, intelligence, the diplomatic corps, and Command all agree," Kirk said. "I wish it were not true, but it is. All we can do now is try to buy some time. For now, that means protecting the dilithium crystals on Starbase 42 and the deposits below on the planet."

"Can we be sure they are going to come after the crystals?" Giotto asked.

"Given the nature and sheer volume of the security breaches, we have to assume that the Klingons have access to that information. And given the recent setback they suffered with the Orion mine in System 7348 we have to assume that it is a strong possibility. And if there is one thing the admiral has learned from the current situation, it is that the worst-case scenario is often the status quo."

"So we may be a-fighting with a crippled ship," Scotty said. "I need a real starbase to fix her, and a replacement dilithium chamber."

"I know you do," Kirk said, "but we may not have time."

"That soon?" McCoy asked, almost more to himself than as a question.

Kirk only shrugged.

"You know Starbase 42 doesn't even have a descent drydock," Scotty said. "It was designed for the likes of a *Daedalus*-class ship."

"Can't you make it fit?" Kirk asked, knowing that more than likely Scott could squeeze the *Enterprise* into a parking garage if he had to.

"Aye," Scotty said, "but we're goin' to have to reconfigure the drydock lattice to do it."

"Just make it work," Kirk said. "Critical systems first. I need full weapons, screens, and warp drive."

"You got that now," Scotty said. "I just want to make sure all that stays working."

"And let's hope the Klingons give you enough time," Kirk said. "If they cooperate, the admiral will authorize high-speed transport of any replacement components you need."

"Amen to that," McCoy said.

Kirk turned to Spock. "I need you to start setting up long-range scans as soon as we arrive at the starbase. Hook into the base's existing systems if you have to boost range. I want as much warning as I can get if the Klingons come across the border."

Spock nodded and said nothing.

McCoy leaned forward and said, "I will take a look at the starbase hospital and make sure it's ready for...well, for anything."

Kirk nodded. "Talk to the people on the surface to get supplies if you have to."

Kirk then turned to Scotty. "I not only need your crew working to make sure the *Enterprise* is ready, but I need you to assign a crew to get the station's defenses up and running."

"Aye, Captain," Scotty said. "I've already been over the station's schematics. We can get supplies from the planet's surface. We'll get that old station something to defend herself with, I promise you."

"Gentlemen," Kirk said, "let's get to work."

With that his senior crew stood and headed toward the door. He stood and watched them go, knowing that his people would make the most of whatever they had. They would do their best and achieve more than he or anyone else had a right to expect.

Yet the knot in his stomach refused to go away.

It was his intuition again. It was not specific, but he didn't need it to be. He knew what was coming. He just hoped they were ready when it came.

McCoy was the last to leave. As he reached the door, the doctor turned. Kirk could immediately tell that the doctor's mind was on the same thing as his.

McCoy said, "Captain, the Klingons were ready to sacrifice that entire planet and all those Klingon lives to be able to launch their war against us."

Kirk nodded.

"How do we beat an enemy like that? What will it take?"

"We hope it never comes to that, Bones, but if it does we give the fight everything we have."

He paused for a moment before he added, "Then we give a little more."

Chapter Five

"APPROACHING THE STARBASE NOW," Spock announced.

"Magnify," Kirk said.

Immediately, the viewscreen revealed the starbase. Kirk knew it was large, yet there was surprisingly little space traffic around it—just cargo tugs and small maintenance vehicles. The station was an older design. It had a large, central disk-shaped hub that was ringed by two large circular sections. Five equally large "spokes" connected the hub and rings.

It must have been impressive in its day, Kirk thought. Though that day would have been during the early days of the Federation. The station no doubt had been upgraded and refitted a number of times. Inevitably, it had been made obsolete by smaller, better-equipped bases.

The captain could see the drydock facility. It was a traditional lattice design. A part of him resisted the idea of putting the *Enterprise* inside. Though the ship needed repairs, while it was in drydock the *Enterprise* would not be as able to defend herself or the station.

The ship needed to be patrolling the sector, not moored in one place.

Soon enough, Kirk thought. Despite his protests, Scotty was no doubt having the same thoughts and would have the *Enterprise* back out there as fast as possible—or more likely faster. They needed precious little time to do that. He hoped the Klingons would be that accommodating, at least.

A moment later and Kirk heard the turbolift doors open. He turned his head to see Admiral Justman on the bridge—*on my bridge,* Kirk thought with a flash of pride.

Reflexively, Kirk was on his feet.

"At ease, Captain," Justman said.

"I have the base now, Captain," Uhura said.

"On screen, Lieutenant," Kirk said.

The face of a young woman in a gold Starfleet uniform appeared on the screen. She looked nervous and very young.

"This is Lieutenant Crane," she said.

"Is the base commander available?" Kirk said.

"No...the commodore is dead," she said.

"Dead?" Kirk said, noting the surprise on the admiral's face in his peripheral vision.

"Yes, sir, he was murdered. We have not found the responsible party," the lieutenant said.

Her grief was etched in her face.

The admiral stepped forward. "This is Admiral Justman, I'm sorry for your loss," he said. "What is the status of the station?"

"Status is normal, sir," she said.

Except for the fact that an operative who was no doubt working for the Klingons has just murdered the Commodore, Kirk thought.

"I'm glad you are here, sirs," Crane said.

"We will arrive shortly and will help you secure the station and apprehend the commodore's murderer," Justman said.

"Enterprise out," Kirk said.

Spock was standing beside the captain a moment later. "Should we commence with liberty for the crew, Captain?"

"It's more important than ever, Mr. Spock. We need to show a presence on the station. It looks like the station crew will need the show of support. Personnel not qualified for repair work should begin liberty at once. Just make sure that everyone is briefed on the current situation before they beam over."

Lieutenant Commander Giotto turned from his station on the bridge. "Captain, I have assigned a team to help with the investigation on the station," he said.

"Good, who have you got to secure the mine?" Kirk asked.

"I will do it, sir," Giotto said.

Kirk thought for a moment. He did not want his chief of security off the ship and in what might become a deadly battleground. On the other hand, the mine could not be allowed to fall into Klingon hands.

Similarly, the crystals on the station had to be protected as well, but Kirk had his own thoughts on how to do that.

"Good luck, Mr. Giotto. I will be in contact with you from the station," he said.

"Thank you, sir," Giotto said, and was on his way to the turbolift.

"Captain," Justman said. "You and I should beam over as soon as we are in transporter range. I want to inspect the station and be able to evaluate our situation as soon as possible."

"Yes, sir," Kirk said, noting the determination in Justman's eyes. He realized that he was also glad Admiral Justman was there.

When Kell woke he opened his eyes to see that Parrish was already awake and looking at him. She smiled.

"Are you ready for liberty? We'll be arriving at the starbase in less than an hour," she asked. Kell was certain that there was something behind her question.

"Then we should get ready," Kell said.

Her face betrayed surprise, and he knew that she had expected him to refuse. She smiled.

He found that he wished to go with her. And she clearly wished to go with him. He was finished denying truths.

In the dining room, they found the remains of the squad at a table and Sam Fuller at the food server.

"How are you, Jon?" Fuller asked.

"I am well," Kell answered.

"How are *you* feeling, sir? Your injuries?" Kell asked.

"I'm back on active duty. I'm fine, even Dr. McCoy seems to think so," he said.

At the table Kell had the feeling that the chief was studying him. Weeks ago, Kell would have viewed the scrutiny with suspicion. Now he saw it for what it was—concern.

Like the others, Fuller was concerned about him. Like the others and like the doctor, he believed that Kell was blaming himself needlessly for his partner's death.

Fuller had great courage and he had seen the human's honor. Suddenly, Kell felt his shame grow under that gaze.

"There's something I need all of you to know before you go on liberty," Fuller said to the table. "We are going to be on high alert for the duration of our time here, and I do not know how long that time will be."

The chief took a breath before he continued. "Many of you have heard rumors of tensions brewing with the Klingons. There are two things I need to report to you. First, the captain has confirmed that Starfleet is now certain that war between the two powers is imminent. We also have reason to believe that this starbase and the planet below may be the target of a Klingon raid. There is a dilithium mine on the surface and we expect that the Klingons may try to replace the crystals they lost in the 7348 incident."

Kell was amazed that the Federation knew or had deduced so much of the Empire's plans.

"The Klingons were definitely behind the mine, then, sir?" Parrish asked.

Fuller nodded. "Lieutenant Commander Giotto found definitive proof of Klingon involvement in the operation," he said.

There was silence at the table as the squad absorbed

this. Kell himself had been surprised to learn what Klingon High Command had planned to do.

If he could not understand what his own people could be capable of, how could these humans?

"And finally," Fuller said, "the commander of the starbase has been murdered and his killer is at large on the base. We are there to show support to the base crew and keep our eyes open. We will also be taking on new crew at the starbase. I have requested only experienced officers to add to the squad."

Fuller glanced quickly at Kell and Parrish.

"Anderson, Parrish, I know you both lost partners and roommates recently. Usually I like to wait before reassigning to give you some time, but the word from the captain is that we will have to be at full capacity and combat ready at all times. All I can promise you is that we will try to pair you with people who can hold up their ends."

Kell was uncomfortable with the idea of sharing living quarters with another human, but he could see it could not be helped.

When Fuller got up he said, "Try to stay out of trouble on the starbase this time." Then he smiled grimly and left.

By unspoken agreement, Kell, Parrish, Clark, and Jawer got up and moved as a group toward the door, then on to the transporter room.

They had a short wait for the transporter then they found themselves on the transporter pad on the starbase. The base transporter room had a large window that revealed the *Enterprise* in a drydock above the plane of the station. The planet must be below the level of the window, Kell realized, because he could not see it.

Checking the transporter-room diagrams, Kell got his first look at what the starbase looked like from the outside. It had a large central hub and five spokes that radiated from it. Connecting the spokes were two outer rings, one that was at the spokes' midway point and one that they terminated into.

The hub and double ring was an interesting design and, Kell noted, an aesthetically pleasing one. He had found that humans often made decisions based partly or sometimes wholly on aesthetics. At first, he had thought that it was a sign of their weakness. Now he saw it for what it was, simply part of what they were.

"Even battered, she's still beautiful," Jawer said, pointing to the *Enterprise.*

"Yes," Kell found himself saying.

"Where to first?" Clark asked.

"How about the Starfleet Canteen? It meets liberty guidelines for approved recreation," Parrish said with a slight smile.

Kell found himself returning the smile, remembering the last time they had gone on liberty together—when Benitez and Sobel were still alive. They had escaped both the angry Nausicaans and the starbase brig virtually unscathed.

Since everyone was in agreement, they headed out of the transporter room. As they left the room, Kell's communicator beeped. He flipped it open.

"Anderson here," he said.

"Jon Anderson," the operator's voice said, "You have a live, personal transmission waiting for you in the communications center."

For a moment Kell did not understand. Who would be communicating with him via a live transmission on the starbase?

"I repeat," the voice in his communicator said. "You have a live—"

"Thank you," Kell said, flipping it shut.

If someone from the ship wanted to reach him, they would simply use the communicator. The only others who might try to contact him might be someone from Klingon Command. It was even possible that it was a friend or family member of the real Jon Anderson.

"What is it?" Parrish asked him.

"I have a transmission waiting for me in the communications center," he said. "I will meet you in the canteen."

Jon took a turbolift to the communications center and reached it minutes later. Back in the corridor, he realized there was something odd about this starbase. Like the previous two starbases that Kell had seen it was, for the humans, fairly utilitarian in its construction. However, unlike the other starbases, it was sparsely populated, and Kell realized that there were almost no civilians on board.

Because the starbase was scheduled for decommissioning, Kell understood why there would be fewer people there. However, there should be more civilians because of that. They were preparing for an attack, he realized.

At the communications center, he saw banks of viewers in small cubicles. He saw a Starfleet attendant at the desk and was approaching when a starbase security officer called out to him and said, "Jon, there you are."

The officer approached and Kell was immediately on his guard.

The human was smiling as he reached out his hand. Kell returned the smile and the handshake. The human was of medium height and wore the red tunic of base security.

Suddenly, he realized that this person must somehow have known Jon Anderson, the real Jon Anderson who no doubt had died months ago at the hands of his Klingon interrogators.

Kell realized that his mission and his life would likely end right here unless he killed the man in front of him. A few weeks ago, he would not have hesitated, but Kell realized that he would not do it now.

He would accept the consequences of his own treachery. It shamed him that his squad and Fuller and Parrish and Kirk would learn the truth, but he would not sacrifice the life of another person to maintain his own deception.

"Let's talk outside," the human said, and Kell followed him into the corridor.

"How do I know you?" Kell said.

"I'm Alan, Alan Port," the human said, leading Kell to a remote part of the corridor where they could speak undisturbed. "I am also as *betleH 'etlh,* or The Blade of the *Bat'leth,* like you are, *Jon Anderson.*"

Then Jon understood. "How did you locate me?" he asked. After the incident in the Orion mine and his confrontation with the High Commander, his Klingon superiors would think he was dead.

"There is another of our blood on board," Port said. "He is an engineer and has set the transporter controls to alert us when a Klingon brother arrives. You came on the *Enterprise?*"

"Yes," Kell said.

"You must have done much for the Empire if the ship is in drydock. They do not suspect you?" Port said.

Kell shook his head.

"It is pitifully easy to earn their trust," Port said.

It was easy, Kell knew, but this Klingon in front of him had not seen the truth there: that the trust they offered each other was a strength, not a weakness.

Kell was standing in front of one of his own blood and realized that this Klingon was more alien to him than the humans he had served with these past weeks.

And yet, to the humans he was alien, a being who had deceived them and they could never accept. A Klingon. A monster.

"There is much to celebrate, brother," Port said. "A Klingon warship is on its way here now."

"Has the war begun?" Kell asked.

Port shook his head. "But there is something on the surface that the Empire needs," he said. "The Earthers have been secretly mining dilithium crystals there for months. I have made my report and now the Empire will have them."

Kell knew this, but he was surprised that this Port had been able to get the information to the Empire.

"How soon?" Kell asked.

"I do not know, but it could be any time," Port said. "I was concerned when I heard that the *Enterprise* was on its way, until I heard that she had been damaged by an encounter with a Klingon vessel," Port said with pride. "I see that it will be in no position to fight while in drydock," he added. "Now our warriors can finish the work on that ship and take the crystals. It will be a great day for the Empire."

Port grasped him firmly on the shoulder. "With a Klingon ship attacking and three Klingon warriors among them, the Earthers will fall quickly."

As a group of officers approached, Port lowered his voice and said, "We will speak again. Wait for my signal."

Then Port hurried down the corridor.

Kell headed for the turbolift. He had vowed to serve the ship, the humans he served with, and the Federation until he died or was exposed. He had vowed to do it to honor the man he had murdered.

Now, to keep that vow, he would have to take arms against Klingons.

Kell hurried to the turbolift. He suddenly wanted to be in the company of the honorable humans of his squad.

And in what might well be the last days or even hours of his life he also found that he wished for Parrish's company.

Chapter Six

WHEN THE transporter effect cleared, Kirk looked out at the starbase transporter room. Along with the transporter operator, Lieutenant Crane and a small security team were waiting for them.

She stepped forward immediately and said, "It's an honor, Admiral Justman, Captain Kirk."

"At ease, Lieutenant," Justman said. "Again, I'm sorry about Commodore Williams, he was a good man."

"Thank you, sir. And thank you, Captain, for sending over your security people. Chief Fuller is already at work with our people who have been looking into the commodore's murder. And we are coordinating with Security Chief Giotto on the surface. And, Captain, your chief engineer is on his way. We have prepared a report on the status of station resources and an inventory of available components."

Kirk could see that the lieutenant was nervous, but that didn't stop her from doing her job, even in extreme circumstances after she had suddenly lost her commander. The service tested some young officers harder and earlier than others. A young Lieutenant Justman had been tested that way at the Battle of Donatu V and had done the impossible.

"Lieutenant," Justman said, "this is my adjunct, Lieutenant West, as well as Mr. Spock, first officer on board the *Enterprise,* and Security Section Chief Brantley."

Crane nodded; then the admiral looked at the young lieutenant expectantly for a moment. She returned the look, realized she had forgotten something, and said, "Admiral, it is my pleasure to formally turn over command of the station to you."

"Thank you, Lieutenant," Justman said. "Have your people begun the work I ordered?"

"Yes," she said, "they are routing all command protocols to your command post. It will have nearly all the functions of auxiliary control but it is in a different sector of the station, as you requested. We have chosen a place for you in the middle ring."

Kirk approved. The admiral was thinking ahead already. In the event of an attack, station defenses and other command protocols could be controlled from auxiliary control, or the admiral's command post.

"Where are we now?" Justman asked.

"We are in the outer ring," she said. "The station was built before transporters were in general use for personnel transport, so the transporter rooms tend to be in out-

of-the way places. It is just a short turbolift ride
to...What would you like to inspect first? The control
center or your command post?"

"I assume the command post would be closer for us,"
Justman said. Crane nodded, and the admiral said,
"Let's check in there first. Where are you keeping the
store of dilithium?"

"The control room, sir. It is the most secure portion of
the station, in the central hub."

"That will be our next stop, then," Justman said.
"Have you prepared the weapons status report?"

"Yes, sir," Crane said.

Kirk was pleased. It looked like the station was under
control. As long as the mine and the dilithium on the station were secure, they had already achieved their most
important mission objectives. And if Scotty got the *Enterprise* fully operational quickly, they might have a
chance.

Lieutenant Kyle watched as Mr. Scott operated the
controls with practiced ease. The travel pod lifted off
from the shuttlebay deck and out into space. The *Enterprise* did not have the pods, but Mr. Scott had requested
one from the station.

The commander piloted them out into space and took
them out past the drydock lattice. The view was impressive. Kyle could see the *Enterprise* illuminated by the
drydock work lights and the site stunned him.

The lattice itself had its own beauty. It formed a rec-
tangular box around the ship, with openings in the front
and back. In fact, because of the size of the *Enterprise,*

the warp nacelles extended past the lattice by fifteen meters.

The lattice was made up of copper-colored tubing and hexagonal platforms, with enough space between to provide a good view of the ship even from the outside.

Kyle had been on these flybys with Mr. Scott before, and he had wondered more than once if the chief engineer took these flights because of the view of the ship.

"There," Mr. Scott said as he took the pod above the drydock lattice. It had been split down the middle and separated to make room for the *Enterprise*'s width. The job looked like it had been a rush and the cuts were not even.

That makes sense, he thought. *They are on emergency footing.*

Mr. Scott checked the physical moorings on the *Enterprise;* then, satisfied, he took them through a break in the lattice. Lyle did not think the opening was big enough for the pod to pass, but Mr. Scott did not flinch as he took them through at full thruster speed.

Inside, they headed directly for the rear of the primary hull. In the back of the saucer, Mr. Scott visually inspected the impulse engines.

"Do you see that, laddie?" the chief engineer said.

"No, sir," Kyle said truthfully.

"There, in the reaction exhaust ports," Mr. Scott said, pointing.

"No, sir, I don't see anything," Kyle said.

"Have the station people use portable sensors to test calibration of the reaction emitters. I think we'll find them off a few hundredths of a percent," Mr. Scott said.

The dual emitters that provided the force that drove the ship at impulse speeds had to be carefully calibrated. Any misalignment between the two would degrade performance of the impulse engines and could be a potential danger to the ship.

On the other hand, it should have been impossible to see a misalignment of a few hundredths of a percent with the naked eye. If it was anyone else, Kyle would have dismissed the observation as ridiculous, but because it was Mr. Scott he had no doubt that an on-site examination with portable sensors would show exactly what he said it would.

Kyle decided to take back what he had thought about Mr. Scott taking these trips around the *Enterprise* for any reason other than necessity.

Next, they traveled along the outside and inside of each warp nacelle, carefully inspecting each of the long cylinders. Mr. Scott stopped at the rear of the port nacelle.

He saw the chief engineer studying the intercoolers on the top near the rear of the cylinder. One of them was clearly warped.

"I see it, sir," Kyle said. "The stellar flare?"

"Aye," Mr. Scott said.

"Will the station have a replacement?" Kyle asked.

"No, but we might be able to put one together if their manufacturing plant is fully functional."

Scott piloted the pod out of the rear of drydock lattice and toward the station.

"Let's take a look at what they have for us," Mr. Scott

Kevin Ryan

said, shooting Kyle a look. The lieutenant realized that he was staring, openmouthed, at the *Enterprise*. "We canna stay out her forever admirin' the ship."

"Can they detect us?" Koloth said.

"We are entering the edge of their sensor range now," the sensor operator said.

"Good," Koloth said. "The Earthers' fear will begin to work on them soon."

Karel checked his tactical readouts. The station had just appeared. A few moments later the smaller *Enterprise* appeared on the screen as well.

The range was far too great for even the *D'k tahg*'s great weapons. Nevertheless, Karel locked the disruptors on target and his blood burned a little hotter.

Karel had spent months in the port disruptor room as a cooling-systems operator and then as a commander. He knew very well what destruction the ship's disruptors could wreak on a vessel or a space station at close range. The torpedoes were equally destructive.

He looked forward to testing the limits of both weapons systems very soon.

If both ship and station were truly incapacitated, the victory would be less sweet, but he would have vengeance against the Earthers who had taken his father and his brother.

A damaged starship and an old starbase would not quell his blood's thirst for revenge, but Karel decided that they would be an excellent start.

As if reading his mind, Koloth appeared behind Karel and said, "You will have your vengeance. But before we destroy them, we must take the dilithium they are hoarding on the planet's surface and, no doubt, on the starbase. Then your weapons will do their work.

"We will board and take the station first; then the planet and its crystals will be ours," Koloth added.

"Then let me lead one of the boarding parties," Karel said. "I would have the Earthers taste my blade."

"I would rather not risk you," Koloth said frankly. "There is much we can do together."

"And I will gladly serve with you, but first I would take the vengeance that is my right," Karel said.

"You have served me well and I know you serve the Empire above all," Koloth said. "Take the first boarding party. They are collecting in the transporter room now."

"Thank you, Captain, for that honor," Karel said.

"I expect you to come back and personally blast that ship and station out of space," Koloth said as Karel turned to go.

"It will be an honor that I will relish," Karel said.

Then Karel left the bridge and headed for the transporter room, his blood burning hotter with every step. Vengeance was so near he could nearly smell it.

A few moments later he stepped into his quarters and picked up his *mek'leth* and strapped it to his waist. Then he fastened his *d'k tahg* to the same belt.

Both blades had been his father's, and he vowed that both would taste Earther blood this day. He made the vow to his honored father and to his honored brother. He made it to Kahless and made it on his own honor.

Finally, he grabbed his disruptor and made sure it was at full power, and then he stepped back into the corridor and was at the transporter room a few moments later.

The strike force was assembled; he was pleased to see Klingons from his disruptor room team there. Torg, who had worked side by side with Karel, smiled when he saw his former commander.

Then a large Klingon near the front turned around, and for the first time since they had battled nearly to the death, Karel was face-to-face with Gash, his own former commander.

The large Klingon's right eye, or what was left of it, was now covered by a metal patch that was bolted in place.

His one good eye studied Karel for a moment; then the Klingon nodded once and turned away.

Koloth had said that Gash would be put to better use as a fighter than a weapons room commander. Karel agreed, and he hoped that Gash did too.

He had come to fight Earthers, not other Klingons.

Yet he would not worry. He would not let anyone stand in the way of his vengeance, be they Earther or a large Klingon named Gash.

Chapter Seven

WEST ENTERED THE ROOM ahead of the admiral. Only after he had done it did he realize that it had been a protective gesture. He also found that he was studying the officers around him very carefully.

There were technicians inside, installing computers and working inside open control panels. Any one of them might be working for the Klingons.

Lieutenant Crane was attractive and just a couple of years older than himself, but West found that he could not stop assessing her as a possible threat to security and to the admiral.

He would have liked to dismiss the thought as frivolous, but he had seen a young yeoman he had thought he knew try to kill Admiral Justman. And the station's commander had just been murdered. There was an operative still on board somewhere.

"This area used to be a communications hub for the station," Crane said. "So all of the circuits we need for your command-post operations are routed through here."

The admiral nodded as Kirk and Mr. Spock inspected the equipment. West noticed that Security Chief Brantley was watching the room carefully, as if he was also assessing everyone in it as a possible threat.

"We should have all of the equipment operational by the end of the day," Crane continued.

The station crew was performing efficiently under difficult circumstances, West noted. If they could find the operative—or operatives, he realized—quickly, perhaps they would be able to secure the station against possible attack.

West stayed close to Justman as the admiral performed his own inspection. The lieutenant noted that the computer equipment would be adequate and the databanks would have everything he needed—though he had brought most of what he needed to continue his work.

He had found a number of promising lines of research, though he had yet to translate them into possible strategies and tactics for use against Klingon ships and personnel in combat.

He found that Klingons believed very strongly in the inevitability of their own victory. And they did not seem to respond well to serious setbacks. And while it was well known that the Klingons did not take prisoners, most people in Starfleet did not know that they had serious social taboos against being taken prisoner themselves.

Those things, combined with the importance to many

of them to seek a death in battle over capture could be exploited by Starfleet in combat situations.

The work was not finished and what he had were notions, not even full-fledged thoughts, but they were a start. All he would need was time.

"What is your weapons status?" the admiral asked Lieutenant Crane.

"We have phasers and shields online, but they are long past being due for upgrades," she said. "We also have some old-style phase cannons."

"Photon torpedoes?" the admiral asked.

"We have the capability but no torpedoes," she said, clearly embarrassed.

"Our chief engineer can work with your manufacturing people to construct torpedoes," Kirk said. Then, as if he was anticipating her next remark, he added, "And we can train your people in the torpedo room, if necessary."

"Thank you," the lieutenant said, giving Kirk a grim smile. "This decommissioning has been coming for years. The base was promised to the civilian authorities on the surface years before the dilithium was discovered. Since then, the civilian government has made continued cooperation with our mining operation contingent on the decommissioning of this base on schedule. As a result, base defenses have not been a priority."

West understood the need for Starfleet to be sensitive to the needs of the civilian population, but things would have to change here. Even if the base and planet survived the immediate crisis intact, it was in too important a strategic position for Starfleet to give it up.

No doubt, Starbase 42 and all others within close

proximity of the Klingon/Federation border would become extremely important in the weeks and months to come. He was certain that in a short time the base would be boasting state-of-the-art defenses.

The civilian authority on the surface might not like it, but Starfleet was here to stay until the war was won or lost.

The intercom beeped and Crane stepped away to answer it.

Nearly simultaneously, Captain Kirk's communicator beeped.

"Crane, here," she said as Kirk flipped open his communicator.

The voice on the intercom said, "Lieutenant, we have something on long-range scanners. It's a ship." The voice sounded very young and very nervous. West noted that most of the station crew he had encountered was young. He noted the irony of such a young crew manning the final days of what was one of the oldest starbases in the service.

"Klingon?" Crane asked.

"We can't tell yet," the voice said.

Kirk spoke next. "It's the Klingons. They're coming in at high warp and will be here very soon."

The room was quiet for a moment as everyone absorbed that information.

Time, West thought.

Time for repairs to the *Enterprise.*

Time to get their command post operational.

Time to improve the station's defenses.

They had just run out of the thing they needed most.

* * *

"Does the com system work yet?" Kirk asked.

Crane shook her head. "The only operational system here is the computer terminal."

The captain saw that Spock was already at work over the console.

"It is a Klingon battle cruiser, D-7 class," the Vulcan said.

The admiral stepped forward.

"Analyze station phaser power and shield capacity," Justman said. "Compute with known parameters for D-7-class vessel."

Spock continued to look into the viewer for a moment, then looked up. "Station phasers would penetrate the Klingon shield given enough time. However, station shields will undoubtedly fail before that happens."

Kirk had his communicator out. "Lieutenant Uhura," he said.

"Klingon vessel does not respond to hails," came her immediate reply.

"They are not here to talk, Captain," Justman said. "They want the crystals, they will immediately take control of the station and the mine, and then they will take what they want. And, Captain, the Klingons do not take prisoners."

"The *Enterprise*," Kirk said. Even as he said it, however, he knew that there was likely little the ship could do. Both phaser power and shield strength were down because of the compromised warp reactor. Still, the ship had torpedoes.

The admiral nodded and Kirk said, "Uhura, take the ship out of drydock, prepare for battle stations."

Then Kirk thought of something else, "Lieutenant," he said, "where is Mr. Scott?"

"He's in a travel pod on his way to the station," she said.

"Brief him and have him report to the control room when he gets here," Kirk said.

"With the *Enterprise* in the fight, we will have a chance," Justman said. "But we cannot allow the Klingons to get those crystals, either on the surface or on this station, Captain."

"We can seal the mine," Kirk said. "Our security force would not stand against a massive ground attack."

The captain turned to his first officer. "Mr. Spock, do station phasers have the power?"

"Yes," the Vulcan said, without even consulting the computer.

"Do it, Captain," Justman said.

Kirk had his communicator out again. "Mr. Giotto," he said.

"Yes, Captain," Giotto's voice responded.

"The Klingons are on the way," he said. "Evacuate the mine and the surrounding…"

He turned to Spock, who said, "Two kilometers."

"Two kilometers," Kirk continued. "We will seal it with phasers."

"Yes, sir, we will move the people out immediately," Giotto said.

"Report when you are ready," Kirk said. "Kirk out."

"Captain," Justman said. "We need to protect the crystals in the control room at all costs. But as badly as we need them, we cannot let them fall into Klingon hands."

Kirk nodded. He understood.

Justman turned to Lieutenant Crane. "How secure is your control room?"

"Heavy blast doors, it's very secure," she said.

"The control room will become our last fallback position," Justman said. "Our last defensive line. We will protect the crystals at all costs. In the event that the control room falls, the last of us will have to destroy them. As badly as we need them, we cannot let the Klingons have them. Preventing that eventuality is the only way we can buy the Federation the time it needs to prepare a proper defense."

Time, Kirk thought. *That's what this fight has been about since we got here.*

And success in this fight would not be measured against what they gained, but what they prevented. Whatever happened, Kirk was suddenly sure that the cost of that victory today would be very high.

The admiral broke Kirk's reverie.

"Do you have a security team stationed in the control room?" Justman asked Crane.

"Yes," she said, "One squad."

"Kirk," the admiral said. "We need more people there."

Kirk nodded. They needed good people in there. The captain opened his communicator again and said, "Lieutenant Uhura, recall Chief Fuller. We need him and his squad to meet us in the station's control center."

Kell returned to his quarters to find it occupied. The human inside extended his hand and said, "Doug Grad, I'm your new roommate."

The Klingon shook the human's hand.

"You served at 1324?" Grad asked.

"Yes," Kell said.

"Then it's an honor. I've seen the reports, that was amazing work," the human said.

"Is this your first assignment?" Kell asked.

"No, don't worry. I'm not completely green. I was posted to the starbase six months ago. Before that I spent a year on a small vessel. This is my first time serving on a starship, though," Grad said.

Kell nodded. If he had to have a new partner, he preferred someone who had been tested. If Grad had served for a year and a half in security, he had likely been tested many times over.

Then the human turned around and finished putting his clothing into the dresser.

Well, he doesn't seem to like to talk, that is something, Kell thought.

Kell's communicator beeped and he opened it reflexively. There was silence and then a voice said, "It begins." Then he could hear the circuit close.

For a moment, Kell could not place the voice. Then he realized that it was Alan Port.

A brief moment later, he heard the red-alert klaxon go off.

"Anderson and Grad to the armory," the intercom said.

Kell took a few seconds to grab the circular data tape out of his tricorder. If he could not send the message to his brother, he did not want it found.

Then he and Grad were in the corridor heading for the armory at a run. There, they saw Sam Fuller handing out phaser-2 side arms to the rest of the squad.

Parrish shot him a glance and he saw a female officer with her whom he did not recognize.

"Here's where we stand," Fuller said. "There is a Klingon cruiser headed this way at high warp. They will be here very soon. The *Enterprise* will likely not get out of drydock in time to engage it and we do not think station defenses will hold it up for long," Fuller said. "The reason the Klingons are here is a dilithium mine on the surface of the planet. Lieutenant Commander Giotto is leading a force to secure the mine, while our team will help station security protect the dilithium stores already on the station. It will probably get pretty rough. We will likely be facing a determined, highly trained Klingon boarding party. As well as the saboteurs on the station, whoever they are.

"Ensigns Grad," Fuller said, nodding to Kell's new roommate, "and Clancy," he said to the female next to Parrish. "Welcome aboard. Now, let's get to the transporter room."

Chapter Eight

MR. SCOTT'S FACE was set as he turned to Kyle and said, "There is a Klingon cruiser on its way."

Kyle felt his heart sink in his chest. "How long?" he asked.

"Not long enough," the chief engineer said.

Kyle had been sure that Mr. Scott would work a miracle, that the captain would do something, that they would have some time....

The lieutenant noted that Mr. Scott was still piloting the travel pod toward the station, which was looming larger and larger in the window every second.

"Can we return to the ship?" Kyle said.

"Captain's orders," Scott said. "He wants me at the station's control center."

"But the ship?" Kyle said.

"There are other priorities here, son. The Klingons canna get ahold of those crystals," Mr. Scott said.

"But sir—" Kyle began, but cut himself off.

He was going to ask what would happen to the *Enterprise*. How they were going to manage to take it into battle in its current condition?

"We go where we're needed," Scott said, his own concern written plainly on his face. "The captain has ordered Uhura to take the ship out of drydock. The *Enterprise* will be in the fight. Wc are going to have to help defend the station, until the captain says otherwise."

Without Mr. Scott there to hold it together, the *Enterprise* would not last long against a Klingon cruiser. Even with Mr. Scott there, it would still be a short fight.

Kyle kept this thought to himself. He kept his attention focused on the station. He could already see the maintenance airlocks. They would be there in less than a minute.

Suddenly, there was something wrong with the station. The lights that shone through the open windows flickered a few times and then steadied—though much less brightly.

And there was something else—the large red dome that Kyle could just make out at the bottom of the station was no longer red. It was completely dark.

"Mr. Scott…" Kyle began.

"I see it, laddie, the station just lost its warp reactor," Scott said, his voice grim and relaying none of the panic that Kyle felt rising in his own throat.

He forced it back by sheer will, taking strength from Mr. Scott's determined stare at the station and the docking bay that was now seconds away.

As bad as things had been just seconds ago, Lieutenant Kyle knew they had just gotten much worse.

"Status of the moorings?" Uhura called out.

"Drydock tractor systems off," the acting science officer replied. "Starbase crews are removing the physical moorings and umbilicals now."

That was the most time-consuming part of leaving a spacedock, Uhura knew. Of course, it had never been designed to be a quick process. As far as the lieutenant knew, there was no such thing as an emergency procedure for what they were doing.

She turned the command chair to the communications station where Perez was working. "Tell the station crews to withdraw immediately, using emergency thrusters on their packs and in their work bees."

"Yes, sir," Perez said.

It would take precious time, but much less than it would to remove the moorings manually. Of course, the moorings were still a problem.

"Let me know when we have an all-clear," Uhura said, and Perez nodded.

Time ticked by, precious seconds.

"Status," Uhura asked.

"Shields now powered up to their current maximum, fifty-eight percent," the acting science officer said. "Phasers at forty-seven percent power."

Uhura said a silent thanks to Mr. Scott, who had insisted on keeping the ship's warp core online, in spite of Starfleet regulations, which called for the warp systems to be shut off while a ship was in dock.

The *Enterprise*'s warp reactor had been operating at minimal power, but had powered up very quickly. Their shields and weapons power seemed pitifully weak given the circumstances, but without the power of the warp core, they would be in a far worse position.

"All clear," Perez announced.

Uhura knew that meant that the repair crews in work bees and environmental suits were now out of danger.

"Blow the moorings and umbilicals," she said. A moment later, she felt a tremor reverberate through the deck. Mr. Scott would be furious when he surveyed the damage caused by the explosive bolts necessary for the emergency separation. On the other hand, if the *Enterprise* survived the next few hours, she would gladly endure his wrath.

Then she gave the order, an order that was virtually always reserved for the captain of a ship that was in drydock. "Ahead, full thruster speed," she said.

"According to the computer, the station's warp core was just turned off," Spock announced, his calm tone belying the gravity of what he had just said.

"Off?!" Justman said, shouting for the first time since the admiral had boarded the *Enterprise*.

Kirk knew all too well what that meant.

"The system has been turned off. Estimated restart time is six hours, forty-three minutes," Spock replied.

"We do not have *one* hour!" Justman said, the frustration written on his face.

Lieutenant Crane returned from the intercom to say, "We cannot reach the engineering decks."

"Sabotage," Lieutenant West said.

It was Kirk's first thought as well.

"The person or persons who murdered your commander are still at work," West continued.

"And working with the Klingons," Justman said.

Scotty, Kirk thought, an idea already forming in his head. Whatever happened, he needed his chief engineer safe.

"Chief Brantley, take one of the station guards and rendezvous with Mr. Scott and Lieutenant Kyle at their docking port. Make sure they get to the control center."

"Yes, sir," Brantley said, already heading out the door with one of Crane's people right behind him.

"We need to get to the control room," Kirk said. "There is very little we can do here."

"Not yet, Captain," Justman said. "We need to seal that mine. Whatever happens in the next few hours on this station, the Klingons cannot take possession of any of the crystals on the surface."

"Lieutenant Commander Giotto reports that the area around the mine has been evacuated," the Vulcan said.

"Weapons status with the warp core down?" Justman asked.

Before the Vulcan could check his computer, Lieutenant Crane stepped forward. Just as she did, the station's lights brightened—not to their former level, but brighter than they had been since the warp reactor went offline.

"Practically none, sir," Crane said. "That was the fusion reactors coming online. The problem is that they were not upgraded when the new shields and phasers were added. The warp core is their only source of power. The only weapons system that we can run from the fusion reactors or battery power are the phase cannons. They are operational but I don't think their power will be sufficient."

"Insufficient by a factor of ten," Spock added.

"The *Enterprise?*" Justman asked.

"She is out of drydock," Spock said. "But current phaser power would also be insufficient," Spock said.

Damn, Kirk thought. This situation was changing for the worse by the minute.

Then the beginnings of an idea struck him. He had his communicator in his hand before it was fully formed.

"Kirk to Giotto," he said.

"Giotto here, sir," came the reply.

"Mr. Giotto, we're having a problem with power up here. Do you have something you can use for charges in the mine?"

There was silence at the other end. Then: "There are some canisters of kirilium that we could set near the surface. I'll need about five minutes to set them up and get my people clear."

"Let me know when you're ready. Kirk out," the captain said, closing his communicator. He turned to the admiral and said, "There is one more thing that we can do."

"You are referring to Mr. Spock's intermix formula that will allow a cold start of a warp reactor."

"Yes," Kirk said. "We might be able to get the warp core back online soon enough to do some good."

"If I remember the report from the last time you tried that," Justman said, frowning, "there were some pretty nasty temporal side effects."

Kirk was impressed. Sometimes he wondered if anyone back at headquarters actually read his reports. It was clear that Admiral Justman had.

"There were, but I think with the refinements Mr. Spock has done in the formula and process we can do it without the side effects." Kirk turned to Spock.

"Theoretically," the Vulcan said. "I would have to recalculate, factoring in the specifications of the station's warp core, which I have already begun."

"Could we can use the temporal side effects to buy ourselves some more of what we need most, time?" Justman said.

Spock shook his head. "That would likely be more dangerous than any other course. And much of the temporal phenomenon that the *Enterprise* experienced was due to the ship's close proximity to the large gravity well of a star."

"Let's do it, then, but first let's take care of the mine," Justman said.

As if at the admiral's command, Kirk's communicator beeped.

"Kirk here," he said.

"Giotto here," said the security chief's voice. "We are heading away from the mine in a transport now."

There was silence for a few seconds, and then Giotto said, "We are out of range, sir."

Justman spoke immediately and said, "Lieutenant Crane, have your people target the mine."

"Yes, sir," Crane said, and then she repeated the order into the intercom.

Kirk shook his head. This was no way to run a defensive operation. They needed the resources of the control center.

"Ready, sir," Crane reported a moment later.

"Fire cannons," Justman said.

They were cut off in the unfinished command center; there was no viewer and no immediate tactical report. Kirk and the others simply waited until Crane said, "A hit, sir."

"Mr. Spock?" Kirk asked.

The Vulcan looked up from his science station viewer.

"The mine is sealed," he said.

"How secure is it?" the admiral asked.

"Completely," Spock said. "I estimate it will take the Federation engineers three months and six days to re-open it."

"The Klingons will not be pleased," Kirk said.

"No, if they try holding this place long enough to re-open the mine, we will have a full-scale war," Justman said. "And without those crystals, I don't think they are ready either. I think we just bought ourselves some time."

"I don't know about us," Kirk said, "but at least we got more time for the Federation to prepare."

Justman nodded. "We are still facing a Klingon cruiser with reserve power and a damaged starship. But we have succeeded in one of our two most important mission objectives. Now we just have to make sure that the Klingons do not get the crystals on this station."

Kirk nodded. He had also heard what the admiral was not saying but was clearly thinking. Succeeding in both mission objectives did not require that any of them survive the coming encounter with the Klingons.

Chapter Nine

"SENSORS ARE MALFUNCTIONING," the Vulcan said, as calmly as if he were reporting the weather.

Lieutenant West had never met a Vulcan before, but from what he saw, much of what he had heard was true. Mr. Spock appeared extremely intelligent and completely without feeling. In fact, he radiated a coldness that made West uncomfortable.

"Sir," Lieutenant Crane said. "Turbolifts are out."

"It's time to get moving, Captain," the admiral said, heading for the door.

"Wait, sir," Lieutenant Basso said. "Here," she said, as she handed one phaser-2 side arm to the admiral and another to West.

For a moment, West considered not taking it. He was a xenoanthropologist, a scientist, not a soldier. At the

Academy, he had taken the required phaser and weapons training and then swore off using them.

He had intentionally chosen a field of study that would make sure he kept that vow.

That was weeks ago. A lifetime ago.

He knew things now he could not forget. He knew about Klingons and he knew that there would be no non-combatants in this fight. There would only be victors and vanquished.

He knew the Klingons did not take prisoners.

Then he realized that he had made the decision to act when he woke up in the starbase hospital bed. He had made the decision when he told the admiral that he wanted to use his scientific talents and education to help defeat the Federation's enemies.

West took the phaser and watched the admiral do the same.

"The Klingons will want to board the station and take us in close combat. For what it's worth, they think their victory is inevitable," West said. "The result of this overconfidence is that they don't react well to setbacks and surprises."

"Then we will have to surprise them," Kirk said.

The group was quickly in the corridor and on the move. West watched Admiral Justman take the lead with Kirk beside him.

More than once, West had wondered what the admiral was like as a young commander. He had read the reports and heard some of the tales from the admiral's own lips.

But until he had seen Captain Kirk in action, he had not really understood. Watching the two men, West felt an irrational sense of optimism and gripped the phaser tightly in his hand.

Lieutenant Uhura studied the viewscreen, willing the Klingon ship to show itself, but the screen showed nothing but the starfield. Tracking a ship traveling at high warp from a close distance was a tricky proposition at best.

With the *Enterprise* and the station's sensors working together they had had a reasonable fix on the Klingon ship. But with the station's sensors out, they were chasing sensor ghosts—very nearby sensor ghosts.

"Phaser status?" she called out.

There was no immediate reply from the acting science officer. After a few seconds, she turned around and said, "Report."

"This doesn't make sense," the officer said. "A moment ago, I was showing sixty-seven percent and rising. Now..."

Then Uhura felt a definite tremor in the deck.

"Get security down to engineering," she called out an instant before the emergency lights started lighting up on control panels throughout the bridge. Uhura jumped to her feet.

"Seal off the engineering deck and get me the captain!" A moment later acting Communications Officer Perez said, "I have the captain."

"Captain," Uhura said. "We have a problem. The ship's warp engines have been turned off."

"Do you have the saboteur?" Kirk asked.

Turning her head, Uhura watched Perez at work. Then the lieutenant said, "Security reports that they have a technician from the starbase cornered…he's fled into one of the warp nacelle accessways."

"Does he have any weapons or explosives?" Uhura asked immediately.

"I want him taken alive," Kirk's voice said.

"No weapons," Perez said, "And security teams are exercising extreme caution."

There was a few seconds of silence, and then Perez said, "The saboteur has thrown himself into the plasma stream."

She turned to Uhura and said, "He's gone, sir."

"The Klingons have come out of warp," the acting science officer said. "They're here, sir."

"We don't have much power for phasers, but we have torpedoes, Captain," Uhura said.

"Is the Klingon ship making any hostile movements toward the *Enterprise?*" Kirk asked.

"No, they are ignoring us and taking position near the station," the acting science officer said. "They have engaged tractor beam and are powering up their transporters."

"What is your position?" Kirk asked.

"We are just outside the drydock, sir," she replied.

"Good," Kirk said. "Make no hostile moves toward the Klingon cruisers. Let them think the *Enterprise* is incapacitated. I'm told they think their victory is inevitable. Let's keep the *Enterprise* in reserve to give them a surprise later. I will reroute Mr. Scott to you to get the warp engines back online. Kirk out."

Uhura gave the appropriate orders and sat heavily in her command chair. The captain's voice maintained its usual confident tone. But Uhura knew that the captain would soon be fighting an overwhelming number of Klingons in close quarters.

Yet the captain would still have a better chance than *Enterprise* would have against the Klingon ship while they had little power and virtually no shields.

There was nothing she or the *Enterprise* could do but wait.

Well, not quite nothing.

Uhura turned to the science station and said, "Have engineering vent some coolant from the mooring holes. Let them think we're hurting."

It wasn't much, but the Klingon ship's sensors would read their warp drive as inactive and would see coolant streaming from their open moorings.

Though using the explosive bolts to escape the moorings had caused some damage, Uhura knew it was primarily cosmetic. Yet to the Klingons, it would look like they had severely damaged themselves trying to blast out of drydock.

Let them think it, Uhura thought. *Let them think we are dead in space.*

"Photon torpedo status?" she asked.

"Armed, ready, and targeted at the Klingon vessel," the tactical officer on duty said.

Yes, the Klingons would likely underestimate the *Enterprise* in its current condition. She very much looked forward to correcting their view.

Kirk conducted his conversation with Uhura on the run, and then stopped to make his report to the admiral, whose face betrayed no emotion. He immediately turned to Lieutenant Crane and said, "The Klingons will be boarding immediately. Deploy your people to concentrate on defending the control center."

As Crane opened her own communicator, Justman turned to Kirk.

"We have to get to the control center and quickly," he said. "We'll rendezvous with the others on the way. If your chief engineer can get back to the *Enterprise*, how long will it take him to get the engines back online?"

Kirk turned to Spock, who said, "With the new calculations already in the ship's computer banks, less than ten minutes."

"Do it," Justman said, and then Kirk was on his communicator issuing the new order to Scotty.

Justman then turned his attention to the small group behind him. "Things have been changing quickly on this mission and when the Klingons show up they are likely to get even worse. I'm afraid that I cannot simply ask for your best, I have to ask you for more. We have to win this. The Klingons cannot have the crystals under any circumstances. And if we win the day today and send them packing back to the Empire, we will either stop this war completely or delay it until the Federation is ready."

Then the admiral was running down the station corridor with Kirk and the others at his heels.

Kell, Fuller, and the squad raced to the transporter room and took to the pads. A moment later, Kell and the others materialized in the station's transporter room.

He immediately saw that the station was not at full

power. Emergency lights illuminated the room and the corridor beyond it. The relatively dim light made the station look more deserted.

They headed out into the corridor, and then Fuller made the announcement that a saboteur had turned off the *Enterprise*'s warp drive, rendering it nearly powerless for what would likely be the duration of the fight.

Kell wondered if the saboteur had been Port or his nameless accomplice on the station. It hardly mattered: the Klingon was dead now, and the one who remained would be one more Klingon warrior among the many who would soon be on board the station.

A vibration rocked the deck, then another.

"The station is under attack," Fuller said. "Let's get moving to the rendezvous site."

They took to the corridor at a full run. The turbolifts would have been quicker, but most of them were out thanks to more sabotage from the two Klingon Infiltrators on board. In any case, Kell knew they were vulnerable to failure during an attack, possibly trapping the security force inside.

Since the transporter room was on the station's outer circle, they had to race down one of the large spokes and head toward the rendezvous site in the middle ring of the station. Beyond that, he knew, was the control room, which was in the central hub.

Near the end of the large corridor that ran down the length of the station's spoke Kell saw a large window near the top of the corridor revealing a small section of the central hub. The scale of the structure was enormous, approximately one hundred decks thick.

Now Kell could see Captain Kirk, Mr. Spock, and a small security force waiting by the entrance to middle ring. When they came closer, Kell saw there were two other officers he did not recognize in the group, an older human wearing an admiral's uniform and a young lieutenant.

Chief Fuller conferred with Captain Kirk and the admiral for a moment.

Then Fuller turned to the squad. "Mr. Anderson, Mr. Grad, Mr. Jawer, Mr. Parrish, and Mr. Clancy, you will come with me. We are going to escort Lieutenant Commander Spock to the station's warp reactor, which is in the lower decks of the central hub. He's going to get the power back on."

Then the chief pointed to a station security guard standing next to him. As the human turned around, Fuller said, "Ensign Port here will show us the way."

Port turned and gave Kell a quick but unpleasant smile. So the Klingon Infiltrator lived.

"The rest of you are with me," Captain Kirk said. "We need to make our way to the control room. We have to protect it and its contents at all costs."

Before the captain turned to go, he looked at Chief Fuller and said, "Good luck, Sam."

"You too, sir," Fuller said.

Then the captain took a moment to consider Fuller's squad. "Good luck to all of you," he said.

Kirk drew his phaser and headed down the corridor at a dead run with the others at his heels.

"Move out," Sam Fuller ordered, with Ensign Port beside him. Kell saw a flash of light from above and realized that the Klingon ship had just knocked out the station's shields.

Instead of heading straight to the central hub, the captain and the others raced along the station's middle ring, which circled the hub. Kell did not have to ask why.

If both teams traveled along the same "spoke" and faced an overwhelming Klingon force, both missions would be ended immediately. Splitting up and taking different routes to the hub would increase their chances.

A red-alert klaxon sounded and a voice came from the intercoms warning of an intruder alert.

Fuller drew his own phaser and Kell followed suit as the rest of the squad did as well. Then Kell realized that the Infiltrator Port was holding his own phaser as well, and standing right next to Sam Fuller.

Kell tightened his grip on his own phaser, ready to fire if Port made any threatening motions toward the chief.

He felt a certainty rise within him. He would die before he allowed any harm to come to Fuller, or the others in his squad.

After all of his doubts, he welcomed the clarity that descended over him as he felt the heat of battle. He might have lost his honor, but the call of his ancestors and the call of his blood was strong.

He followed the call as he followed Sam Fuller deeper into the station.

Chapter Ten

LIEUTENANT KYLE could tell by the expression on Mr. Scott's face that something was wrong—something other than the half-dozen serious setbacks they had suffered in the last hour.

"The *Enterprise*'s warp engines have been shut down, laddie. She's a sitting duck out there. The captain wants us to return to the ship to perform a cold restart. Mr. Spock will have to restart the station core by himself."

A moment later, Chief Brantley came running around the corner with a station security guard beside him. "Mr. Scott," Brantley said. "This is Ensign…"

"Briggs," the young man said.

"I received the new orders from the captain. We're going to escort you to the nearest transporter and get you back to the *Enterprise*."

Mr. Scott nodded and said, "Aye, but we may not

need much escorting." He pointed to the cargo transporter right next to the row of maintenance airlocks, one of which they had used to dock the travel pod.

Scott rushed over to the transporter, which Kyle recognized as an older model; in fact, it was older than any other unit he had seen in service.

Mr. Scott manipulated the controls for a minute, then muttered something inaudible under his breath. That particular stream of words was the only Gaelic that Kyle had ever heard the chief engineer use. And Kyle did not need a translator to understand their meaning.

"The unit's been tampered with, the circuits are fried," Scott said.

"Sabotage?" Chief Brantley asked.

The chief engineer nodded.

"Why sabotage the transporters?" Kyle asked with surprise.

"They are an effective weapon in a tactical situation like this one. The Klingons have to lower their shields to transport their warriors over here. With working transporters, we could beam over personnel or explosives."

"We'll have to take the travel pod back to the ship," Mr. Scott said.

"Absolutely not," Brantley said. "Much too dangerous. The Klingons will blast anything that leaves this station. And you are the only one who can restart the warp core, Mr. Scott."

Brantley gestured out the window, which showed the northern pole of the planet and the Klingon cruiser sitting just a few hundred meters away. The *Enterprise* was not in view. Clearly, the Klingons were keeping the station as a buffer between themselves and the *Enterprise,* just in case the starship had any plans of getting into the fight.

Scotty nodded.

Though Kyle knew Scott outranked the security section chief and almost everyone else on the ship, Brantley was responsible for his safety. Thus, until they were back on board the ship, he was in charge.

"Can we find you another transporter?" Brantley said.

"Aye," the chief engineer said. "The transporters on the station were all retrofitted. That means each unit or group of units will probably have their own circuits. Whoever made a mess of this one probably didn't have time to get them all."

Brantley turned to the starbase security officer, Briggs, and said, "Okay, Ensign, where is the nearest transporter?"

"Tha' is a different model than this one," Mr. Scott added.

Briggs thought for just a moment and then said, "Follow me."

Up in the distance, Lieutenant West could see the intersection that told him they had come to the next "spoke" in the station's layout. They would turn left and then be at the core in a few minutes.

The first hint of trouble came when they reached the edge of the intersection. It came in the form of a flash of light that passed less than a meter to his right.

He turned just in time to see one of the station security guards who had been practically next to him go flying backward. Snapping his neck around, he saw the young man lying on the deck, a large hole cut in his chest.

A surprisingly detached part of his mind noted that the man was dead, and then he was moving to the left side of the corridor and flattening himself against the wall along with the others in the group.

The admiral called out for everyone to follow him, and headed left, toward the center of the station. The Klingon fire had come from farther along the curved corridor. The Klingons would no doubt be behind them shortly, but they would at least be heading in the right direction.

West was barely around the corner when disruptor fire came from up ahead of them. This time, no one was hit, but the admiral ordered them to change direction again. A moment later, the entire group was heading along the spoke and away from the central core. They encountered more fire when they crossed the intersection, and this time the admiral, the captain, and the others returned fire.

Then, almost on its own, West's hand swung his own phaser around. The Klingons there had all come far enough along the curved corridor to all become visible. There were perhaps a dozen of them.

West aimed at the center of the group and fired.

It was only later that he realized it was the first time in his life that he had fired a weapon at another living being.

Then they were out of the intersection and racing down the corridor toward the outer ring of the station. It was the wrong direction, but West saw that they had little choice.

They covered the distance to the station's outer ring quickly and turned right. West figured they would try the next spoke and make a straight run for the control center.

But West could feel the seconds ticking by. Even if they reached the central hub, there would no doubt be a concentration of Klingons there. The control center would be one of the first places they would seek out.

Another setback. Another obstacle to a task that already seemed impossible.

The situation must have seemed impossible to Admiral Justman at the Battle of Donatu V, yet he had prevailed.

West kept his eyes on the admiral and kept running.

The lieutenant calculated that they were about halfway around the next section of outer ring when the first disruptor bolts came by.

This time, West dove for the deck and returned fire. The security officers next to him did the same, while the admiral and the captain fired from standing positions against the walls.

West could see the Klingon force from around the curve of the corridor. Just one or two would appear at a time to blast them, and then they would disappear out of sight. Thus, it was impossible to determine the size of the Klingon force there.

However, West knew that the Klingon force behind them was at least ten warriors strong. It would be more if the two forces that would have met at the intersection joined forces, which West thought was likely.

So they couldn't go forward or back. And very shortly they would be caught in the crossfire of two heavily armed Klingon parties.

According to regulations, surrender was recommended in situations where Starfleet personnel were facing overwhelming force. But the Klingons did not take prisoners, at least not for long. And West had learned enough about Klingon interrogation techniques to know that he did not want to learn any more—especially firsthand.

The Klingons had strong social taboos against being taken prisoners themselves; they had particularly little regard for foes who voluntarily gave themselves up.

The admiral called out a cease-fire order and West stayed his phaser. Then Kirk, Justman, and Crane and a few station guards were rushing across the corridor. West and the others on the floor rolled to the left side with them.

"Resume, keep them busy," Justman said.

West and the three security officers carefully sent phaser fire in the direction of the Klingons, keeping it up constantly so the Klingons would not dare peek out from their cover.

Then he heard the admiral's voice say, "Come on."

West was on his feet in an instant and following the admiral and the others through a large door opening that had appeared in the left-hand side of the corridor.

He was one of the last ones in and watched as Lieutenant Crane punched in a security code in the door panel.

"They won't get through here, at least not for a while," she said. "But it won't take them long to figure out where we went."

She turned to two of the starbase security guards and told them to shut the doors to seal off this sector.

"They will be able to access this area from either side, and the doors dividing the airlock sectors are not as strong," she said.

West understood why. To their left were a series of

airlock doors separated by windows that looked out into space and over the planet below. They were on the very outside of the outer ring of the station. The corridor they were in also functioned as a large airlock space.

The heavy door that now protected them from the Klingons outside protected the station from the void of space in case of decompression in one of the smaller airlocks.

Approaching the nearest window, West could see travel pods and work bees attached to the outer airlock. He could also see the Klingon cruiser hanging what seemed like a few hundred meters away from the station and just below them.

"Does the command center have an emergency airlock that we can access with a work bee?" the admiral asked Crane.

"Yes, sir," she said. "But I don't know how far we will get with the Klingon cruiser outside."

Then West heard the sound of disruptor fire pounding against the outside door.

"We'll have to chance it," Justman said. "We won't last long in here. If we split into two groups, we can double our chances of at least one of us getting through."

"We could disable the work bee's acceleration governors," Kirk said. "That would make them more maneuverable and harder to hit."

The captain studied the Klingon ship for a moment as it hung outside the window and then said, "We'll be most vulnerable when we disengage from the station. But as you can see, the Klingon ship has placed itself on a diagonal opposite the *Enterprise* with the station in between. If we can skim the top of the outer ring to the nearest spoke and then travel along the top of the spoke, the Klingon ship won't have an angle of fire unless they move the ship. By then we'd almost be at the central hub and they might not want to risk a full-power disruptor blast so close to the station with so many of their people inside."

The door shook behind them and started to glow red in the center.

The admiral studied the scene himself for a moment and said, "We'll release the other pods and work bees in this sector to give them more targets to track."

West watched in amazement. He was with two of the best tactical minds in the service. A few moments ago, he was wondering how much longer they would have to live. Now he was certain that—between the captain and the admiral—it was the Klingons who were running out of time.

"I think we should split you and Admiral West up," Lieutenant Crane said to Captain Kirk.

"No," West found himself saying forcefully.

The others looked at him in surprise. A moment later, Crane asked, "Why?"

"I doubt anyone in this room is as highly rated a command pilot as Captain Kirk. The admiral will be safest in his pod."

"Surviving this trip will have as much to do with luck as anything else," Justman said.

"I agree with Lieutenant West, Admiral," Crane said.

The admiral seemed about to protest when Captain Kirk said, "Best not to argue, Admiral. We don't have much time."

The admiral nodded. West knew the admiral was right.

It would take more than piloting skill to keep the slow travel pods out of the way of Klingon disruptor fire. On the other hand, it would not hurt. And West was now convinced that the Federation needed Admiral Justman more than ever—for today and for the months to come.

They quickly divided into two groups. The admiral, Kirk, West himself, and two security guards in one pod, and then Crane and four other guards in another. Two of the station guards had technical training and they were immediately put to work disabling the travel pods' acceleration governors.

Then the admiral and Kirk ordered everyone into their pods as the two men ran in opposite directions setting travel pods and work bees to auto-launch.

West waited until the admiral was on his way back to step through the outer door of the small airlock that led into the travel pod. Before he stepped through the inner door and into the pod itself, he spared a look at the main door to the corridor.

The door was glowing red almost all over and a dangerous-looking purple and even white in some places. The door was still holding back the Klingon attack force, but barely.

They had less than a minute, perhaps only seconds. Then Kirk and the admiral were jumping into the pod.

"Governor's disabled," one of the security officers said. And Kirk was immediately at the controls.

"Admiral," West said, pointing his phaser at the outer door of the pod's small airlock. "I have an idea."

The admiral immediately understood and said, "One moment, Captain," as West adjusted his phaser.

Aiming carefully at the outer door's top metal hinge, West fired. The hinge blew off the door immediately. Then he did the same to the bottom hinge with the same results.

Without even checking to see if the door to the corridor was holding, West shut the travel pod's door.

The instant the seal indicator light turned green, the admiral said, "Now, Captain!"

Then West felt a sudden jolt as the travel pod seemed to leap from the station. It slammed his forehead against the rear of the pod, but he barely felt it.

West was certain that his plan had worked. The airlock door that West had blasted open began evacuating the atmosphere of the launch area as soon as the pod launched. When the Klingons burst in from the corridor, they would be sucked into the vacuum created there.

And any Klingons in the corridor for a least a few hundred meters in each direction would be caught inside the safety forcefields that would contain the effect of the hull breach.

How many Klingon lives? Ten? Twenty? Thirty?

At one time West had made a vow never to take another life. Yet he found now that he felt only satisfaction that he had helped, that he had contributed somehow.

He turned forward, carefully grabbing the rear wall to keep on his feet.

Ahead, he could see a work bee in front of them—no doubt one of the empty ones that Kirk and Justman had set for auto-launch.

One moment he saw the small maintenance craft flying in a straight trajectory. The next moment, there was a green flash and the full-power blast of a Klingon disruptor tore through the small craft and there was a brief explosion. Then West could hear small pieces of debris pelting the outside of their work bee.

There was another explosion nearby but West could not see anything but space as Kirk put their craft through a gut-twisting series of maneuvers that West was sure the vehicle's designers never intended.

Then they were skimming the surface of the spoke toward the central hub.

"Justman to Crane," the admiral said.

"Crane here, sir. We're right behind you," said Crane's voice.

"Glad you made it, Lieutenant," Justman said. "Just one more tricky maneuver and we'll see you on the other side of the central hub. You break to the right and we'll break to the left."

"Yes, sir," she replied. "We'll see you on the other side."

The pod moved with surprising speed close to the surface of the station. Still, the seconds ticked by slowly and West knew that the Klingon cruiser might be changing position now to take aim at them. There was no way to tell for sure. The pod did not have sensors and the only window was forward.

If the Klingon ship targeted them, they would have no warning. They would simply disintegrate under its fire.

Yet when the central hub began to loom larger and larger West began to relax. They would make it.

Perhaps the Klingons suspected some trick and thought they were trying to draw it out in the open—into the line of fire of the *Enterprise*.

Whatever their reason, no disruptor fire came.

"Hold on," Kirk said. "We're going to maneuver around the hub now. The Klingons will be able to target us for a few seconds at most."

By that time, West knew, they would be just a few dozen meters from the station's central hub. The Klingons would hardly risk a full-power disruptor blast so close to the station's core. If they hit the station, they would lose warriors and possibly the crystals they sought as well.

"Now," Kirk said, and West felt the pod lurch to one side, twisting into a new arc and shooting upward.

"Admiral—" Crane's voice said over the com system.

Then West saw something impossible on the far right of the window as the travel pod banked right. Another pod, which could only be the one carrying Crane and her team, shot forward tumbling end over end.

Then there was a flash of green energy. It shot out a few meters to the side of the pod, but moved quickly toward the small craft, finally striking it dead-on as it tumbled through space.

For an instant, West was surprised to see that the pod was still intact, then he realized why.

The Klingons would not risk a full-power disruptor blast so close to their prize, but it would take far less than a full-power blast to destroy an unshielded, unprotected travel pod.

He heard shouts from inside the pod on the com system and watched in horror as the craft came apart with what seemed like agonizing slowness. As the audio abruptly died, the pod split into a few large pieces, and for one terrible moment West could see people struggling in the vacuum of space.

"They're gone…" someone said.

Then Kirk executed one of his violent maneuvers and their travel pod shot around the station's central hub.

West sensed they were safe, but felt the sight he had just witnessed embed itself in his stomach like a solid mass.

Seconds later he felt the travel pod snap into an airlock. Then the green indicator light above the door said it was safe to exit.

The admiral hit the button and both inner and outer doors opened. West felt himself being ushered out and was on a catwalk that overlooked a dome below them, perhaps two meters away.

The lieutenant knew that bridges and control rooms often had a double-hull design. The travel pod had just connected with the outer hull and he was now looking down into the inner hull.

They had reached the control center. Amazed, West realized that the whole trip had taken just minutes.

But they had paid a high cost, West realized—Lieutenant Crane and her people. A quick glance at the others told him that they were all having the same thought at the same time.

Then he heard the admiral's voice—its calm but firm tone shaking him out of his thoughts.

"This is far from over. Down the ladder," he said.

West watched the two security guards head down the access ladder that would take them to the control room's floor level less than ten meters blow them. When the two men were on the ladder West reached for it and began climbing down.

Chapter Eleven

"KLINGON SHIP FIRING DISRUPTORS," the science officer said.

"Give me visual," Uhura said.

The viewscreen showed an angle down on the starbase. The Klingon ship was obscured by the station, which was no accident, Uhura knew.

The Klingons no doubt thought they were dead in space, but the Klingon commander was not stupid. He did not want his ship in the *Enterprise*'s line of fire. The Starfleet vessel would have to move first. Thus, the Klingons would have warning before they did. It would prevent the starship from taking advantage of the Klingon cruiser's vulnerability when it lowered its shields to transport warriors to and from the station.

"Sensors!" she called out.

"They are firing at some small craft, I think they are

maintenance vehicles. They have destroyed two, now three. The Klingons have ceased fire."

The screen showed something moving above the surface of one of the spokes of the station.

"Magnify," Uhura said.

Then she could clearly see two travel pods skimming the surface out of the line of fire of the Klingon ship.

"If the Klingon ship moves to intercept, bring us about and fire photon torpedoes," she said.

But the Klingon ship didn't move. As the work bees reached the central hub, a disruptor beam lanced out from below, cutting through the open space and right into one of the travel pods. Then the disruptor beam cut through the people thrown into the void of space.

The captain, Uhura thought as she stood. *It must be the captain trying to get to the control center.*

But which travel pod was his? The one darting around or the one that the entire bridge crew watched come apart before their eyes?

Uhura waited almost a minute before issuing her next order, calculating the time required for the travel pod to dock with the station.

When she spoke, she kept her voice calm by force of will. "Get me the captain."

Seconds ticked by before there was a response. Uhura heard her heart beating loudly in her own ears as the entire bridge crew held their collective breaths.

Finally, Kirk's voice filled the bridge as he said, "Kirk here."

She could not keep the relief out of her voice, "Captain, we were monitoring your situation."

"We're in the control room now. Is Mr. Scott on the *Enterprise?*"

"Not yet, sir," she said.

"Let me know when he arrives. Kirk out."

Uhura sat back into the chair.

And waited.

"Klingons!" Lieutenant Kyle whispered to Chief Engineer Scott, pointing to the right down the corridor.

Section Chief Brantley motioned for Mr. Scott, Kyle, and Ensign Clark to move back into an alcove and held his weapon out.

Kyle could hear the sound of the Klingon boots thudding on the deck plating dozens of meters away. The lieutenant knew they were lucky that the Klingons didn't believe in sneaking around. They just marched, heavy-footed, letting anyone with a good ear know they were coming.

The Klingons were very close now. Kyle was holding his breath and noticed that the others were doing the same. He heard the sound of his own heart pounding in his chest.

As loud as his own heart sounded to his own ears, he was thankful that the sound of the Klingons marching masked its thunderous beating. Gripping his own phaser tightly, Kyle tried to take his cue from Mr. Scott, who was watching alertly but did not seem afraid, merely ready.

Then, as he watched carefully from the temporary safety of the darkened alcove, Kyle saw—for the first time in his life—Klingons, five of them as they passed by. His first thought as he watched them go was that he had expected them to be bigger, both taller and broader, but they looked to be not much bigger than the humans he served with on the *Enterprise.*

Distracted by this thought for a moment, Kyle forgot his own rising fear, and then the Klingons were gone, without having given the small band of Starfleet officers a glance.

Though that was the first time Kyle had seen Klingons on the station, he had heard them more than once. Chief Brantley seemed to think that the Klingons had control over most of the station already. It would be just a matter of time before they controlled the entire starbase.

The captain would hold out as long as anyone could in the control room—and then some. But Kyle knew that the only real hope lay with Mr. Scott and getting him to the *Enterprise.* With the starship's warp power back online, they could give the Klingon ship a surprise, and turn the battle around.

First, they had to get Mr. Scott on board. And the chances were getting slimmer and slimmer as they found it more and more difficult to maneuver in the station with Klingons seemingly all around.

"Clear," Chief Brantley whispered.

The chief motioned that the others should follow him, and he started off at a fast walk down the corridor.

"How far?" Lieutenant Kyle asked.

Section Chief Brantley glanced at Briggs, who said, "The nearest transporter is a cargo unit two decks down and about two hundred meters ahead of us."

"We can go down here," Scott said, stopping and pulling a panel from the wall and setting it aside as quietly as he could. Inside the panel was a maintenance ladder that went down into blackness.

The ladder was a good idea. Kyle had a feeling that very soon the corridors would be impassable.

"I'll go first," Kyle said, trying to make his voice sound confident. Helping keep his commanding officer safe was the least he could do. And without Scott, he was certain that none of them had a chance.

Chief Brantley put a gentle but firm restraining hand on his shoulder.

"Mr. Kyle, you follow me, then Mr. Scott, then Briggs will come last." He faced Briggs directly. "Make sure you close the access panel."

The ensign nodded.

Brantley looked down into the darkness. "I will make sure the corridor is clear. Stay on the ladder until you get my signal."

The group nodded and Brantley started climbing down the ladder.

Kyle slipped his weapon onto his belt and turned to grip the ladder with both hands. Kyle waited a few seconds to make sure the chief was far enough down that he would not step on him.

"The last place I'd like to meet a Klingon is in a dark hole," Kyle said as he started down.

"I'd rather not meet one at all," Briggs said with a grim smile.

As he descended, Kyle heard the sound of weapons fire from somewhere in the station. It could have been above or below them—or a few hundred meters in either direction along the corridor outside.

Or it could have been coming from all of those for all he knew.

As he climbed down, he sincerely hoped that it was not coming from below. The trip seemed to take forever in the near complete darkness that surrounded the ladder, but Kyle calculated that in reality it had to be less than a minute.

There was a light from below. Kyle froze.

The next sound he heard was the chief's voice, which said, "All clear."

Continuing down the ladder, Kyle soon felt the solid deck beneath his feet. He leaned down and came out on another deck, which was completely deserted except for Chief Brantley, who was scanning the corridor carefully.

He was pleased to be in the light again. On the other hand he knew that the brightly lit corridor would give them nowhere to hide.

"One more deck," Brantley said. "Help me find the next ladder accessway."

Kyle moved, hoping that the transporter they found next would be the one to take them home to the *Enterprise*.

At an intersection of the corridors, the Vulcan halted them, turned to Ensign Port, and asked, "Does the central core of the station have a self-powered emergency turbolift that can take us to the engineering decks?"

For a moment, Port looked stricken. Kell knew that he did not want to give the Vulcan an answer; to do so would give assistance to the enemy.

Kevin Ryan

"Ensign?" Spock asked.

Kell watched Port grip his phaser more tightly and he knew the Klingon was calculating his chances against the squad, wondering how many he could hit before someone stopped him.

None, Kell thought as he began to raise his own phaser. *It ends now.*

A blast tore into the wall next to Kell's right before he could fire. He recognized the green flash instantly. *Disruptor fire,* he thought.

Without hesitating, Kell continued his motion and fired past Port and into the corridor where the Klingon warriors were advancing.

"Cover," Fuller shouted, moving quickly to one side of the corridor as the team split up and did the same on either side of the corridor. The support beams that ribbed the walls provided some cover.

Kell found himself and Grad behind one pylon, firing in a nearly continuous stream. Sparing a glance at the rest, he saw Fuller, in position in front of them, with Parrish and her new partner Clancy on the other side, with Spock and Jawer.

Port, however, was still in the corridor. The Klingon who wore the face of a human and the uniform of a starbase security officer clearly did not know which way to go.

To either side of him were the Earthers he was sworn to destroy.

In front of him were Klingons of his blood.

The Klingon's hesitation was momentary and understandable; it would also cost him his life in seconds out in an unprotected position. Fuller noticed Port's position a split second after Kell had himself.

"Port!" Fuller shouted. "Get to cover now!"

Kell saw the smile that told him that the Klingon in the corridor was not going to take another order from an Earther. The proximity of the Klingon force had obviously given him a new sense of purpose.

Port gave Fuller an unpleasant sneer and raised his phaser. Unlike Port, Kell knew his path and did not hesitate.

He redirected his phaser and swung it out to target Port...

...A fraction of a second before the Klingon took a full-power disruptor blast that disintegrated him instantly.

Kell turned his attention back to the battle and kept up his own fire, his phaser finding its own target: a large Klingon warrior. It was the first time he had ever taken a Klingon life, and he found that his blood was quiet, except for its continued call to defeat this enemy.

The Starfleet cause was just, he knew. He also knew that it would be a mistake from which the Klingon Empire would never recover. Even if it won, the stain on the Empire's honor could never be erased.

And the High Command who would sacrifice the lives of a planet full of Klingons to achieve a dishonorable victory would be emboldened by their success. More atrocities would follow, Kell had no doubt.

Perhaps if the Empire failed to get the dilithium, it would delay the coming large-scale attack. Perhaps that attack would never come and more honorable forces in the Empire would prevail.

Kell knew that the future glory of the Empire could come only from Kahless's path to honor. And the followers of Kahless were growing in number every day and every year.

They were the Empire's future.

So Kell followed his blood and followed the lead of Captain Kirk, who had saved Gorath and all of his people.

Kell's phaser found another target. And another.

The others were also making hit after hit. Kell noted that Spock was a particularly good shot, though he went about his work with a calm precision that looked completely alien to Kell, who was caught in the heat of the battle.

Kell fired and fired again.

Yet he could see that the Klingons were still coming. Kell could not see how many there were but he could see that they had already lost more warriors than the small Starfleet team had in their force.

In Kell's time with Starfleet he had never seen them fight against less than overwhelming numbers and overwhelming odds.

He had also never seen them lose, it occurred to him.

Still, as he watched the Klingons advance, he feared that this might be the first time he saw that happen. The battle could not continue long like this. The Klingons would eventually overwhelm them, and Spock would never be able to get the station's power back on.

With the *Enterprise* out of the fight, and the station's defenses without power, even the few brave Starfleet officers with him and with the captain would not be able to stand under the onslaught of a Klingon battle cruiser.

He had to do something, and quickly.

"Sir, I have an idea," someone said. It took Kell a moment for it to register that the words had come from the man next to him, from Ensign Grad.

"What do you need?" Fuller called back.

"Just some cover," Grad said.

"You have it, Ensign," Fuller called out.

Then Grad was on the move.

"Hold your fire!" he called to Spock, Parrish, and Clancy, who were positioned slightly behind him on the other side of the corridor.

Kell and Fuller increased their fire as Parrish and the others held theirs. Grad moved quickly, cutting a diagonal across the wide corridor, and then Kell saw what the human was doing.

The corridor they were in currently ran in a circle around the central hub of the station. To get to the station's core, they would have to head about fifty meters ahead of their position and then turn right on the corridor that cut perpendicularly to theirs and ran to the station's center.

The problem was that the Klingons were perhaps twenty meters ahead of that right turn. The Klingons would no doubt cut down the Starfleet team before they reached the intersection, let alone made the turn.

Grad's plan, if it worked, would cut the Klingons off and give them a clear run to the center of the station.

But to do it, Grad would have to reach the controls for the blast doors that were just a few meters from the Klingon forces' position.

Kell concentrated his fire on the Klingons who would

have the most direct line of fire on Grad. Unfortunately, that was almost all of them.

Still, Grad's zigzagging sprint seemed to be working. He had covered most of the distance to the control panel while the Klingons concentrated the bulk of their fire on the main Starfleet force.

Just a few more meters, Kell thought.

Grad obviously had the same thought, because as a disruptor bolt streaked in the air over his head, the ensign threw himself into the air at the control panel.

A disruptor bolt raced toward Grad and there was an explosion and a great flash of light. For a moment, Kell thought that Grad had disappeared. Then he realized that the bolt had struck the huge, reinforced frame that held the blast doors in place when they were closed.

He saw that Grad was on the floor, intact if not alive.

Then the human stirred. He was cut in a number of places that Kell could see and his left arm hung loosely. But the human was moving, pulling himself forward on his right arm.

When he was directly beneath the control panel, Grad pushed himself to his knees. Then he paused for a breath and swung his right arm at the controls. Just as he started the movement, Kell caught sight of a blast fired at nearly the same moment.

It would be close, very close.

Grad won. His hand slapped the panel a split second before the blast tore into him.

Kell knew that a direct hit with a disruptor set on full was devastating and would almost immediately disintegrate a person.

This was not a direct hit, but it was still more than enough to extinguish Grad's life. The blast caught his left shoulder and tossed the human in the air.

When Grad—or what was left of him—hit the ground, he was still.

The blast doors began closing immediately. They were designed to protect major sections of the station from a major decompression. In just a few seconds, they closed between the two battling forces, and then the Klingons' deadly bolts of energy were cut off.

Fuller fired the next and last shot of the encounter. He blasted the control panel, effectively locking the door.

As soon as that was done, Fuller was heading down the corridor at a run, shouting, "Move out!"

As Kell made the turn toward the station's central core, he said a silent thanks to Ensign Grad, even as he avoided looking at the human's mangled form.

As he ran he remembered that Grad had served in Starfleet for a year and a half. Yet this was how his first day of service as a part of the *Enterprise* crew had ended.

Chapter Twelve

KIRK STUDIED the Klingon cruiser on the control room's main viewscreen.

"The Klingon vessel had not made a move against the *Enterprise,*" Kirk said. "That's something."

As long as the ship was in space, there was still hope that Scotty could get there in time to put the ship back into action.

"My guess is that the Klingon commander is waiting to take care of the ship after he has achieved his objective on the station and has possession of the dilithium crystals," Admiral Justman said from behind him.

"Do you think they expect us to fire on them? Either from the ship or the station?" Kirk asked.

"No, Captain," Lieutenant West said. "A Klingon in our position would fire even low-power weapons, just to strike at his enemy, even if it would mean his immediate destruction."

"Will they get suspicious if we don't do the same?" Kirk asked.

"No at all. In fact, they do not expect us to fight," West said. Then, reading Kirk's quizzical expression, he added, "They consider us a lesser race, a race without much courage. In fact, the term *cowardly* is usually applied to us in communiqués. It is about as big an insult as the Klingons use."

"For now, at least, that thinking is working to our advantage," Justman said.

With one more look at the screen, Kirk turned to the group in the control room.

When Kirk and his team had arrived through the access tunnel they had found four young and scared lieutenants at their posts.

Kirk knew it was easy to underestimate new officers in that position. He remembered that a young and untried Lieutenant Justman had somehow bested three Klingon battle cruisers at Donatu V.

All heads turned to hear a fresh round of disruptor fire slamming into the control center's shields.

"Stations," Justman called out.

The four of the starbase's young lieutenants took their stations. They were under orders to wait there until full power was restored. When the warp core came back online, they needed to be ready to put the shields up immediately and fire the station's weapons, both the relatively low-power phasers and even the old-style phase cannons.

It was not much, but it was all they had to fight back

with. If the *Enterprise* got into the fight, it might even be enough.

What they needed was a weapon, something to do the Klingon vessel real harm.

Of course, Kirk thought. He should have thought of it immediately.

"Admiral, I have an idea," Kirk said.

"Proceed," Justman said. "We don't have much time."

As if to agree with him, the drumming of disruptor fire on the control center's shield intensified.

"Lieutenant," he said to the officer at the sciences station. "How are the Klingons maintaining position?"

"Tractor beam, sir," she said.

"Can you pinpoint where?"

"Yes, sir," she said, calling up an image of the battle cruiser and the station. Then she pointed to a point on the outer ring nearest the Klingon ship.

"Is that anywhere near a shield emitter?" Kirk asked.

"Yes, sir," the science officer replied.

"Ensign," Kirk said to the base security officer who had switched off the travel pod's acceleration governor.

"Yes, sir," he said.

"What is your name?" Kirk asked.

"Marsilii, sir," the young man replied. He was young and was no doubt scared; yet he had performed well under extreme pressure in the travel pod.

"Ensign Marsilii," Kirk said, "you've had some technical training?"

"Yes, sir," the ensign said. "My cross-training was in engineering. I plan on requesting an engineering post for my next assignment."

Kirk nodded. "Could you vent some plasma out of one of the station's shield emitters? I need a strong electromagnetic pulse."

The ensign didn't answer immediately. He first inspected the weapons station, then the engineering panel.

"I...think so, sir. I would have to run some new circuits, but I think I could do it," Marsilii said.

"Then get started," Kirk said.

He turned to the admiral, who said, "You're thinking of hitting them with an EM pulse from the inside, using their own tractor beam as a carrier wave."

Kirk nodded. "You do read the reports," he said.

Justman nodded. "We're already working on an upgrade on shielding of internal circuits so that no one else can use the trick the Orions used on the *Enterprise.*"

"Control room shield down to twenty-seven percent," the lieutenant at the weapons console announced.

"Let's go," Justman said.

Justman led the way to the control center's large blast doors. He hit a switch and the double doors opened with surprising speed.

The admiral stepped through into the perhaps twenty-meter space between the inner blast doors and the outer doors, which were the main entrance into the control room, and the path the Klingons would use.

Kirk and the base security officer took positions behind station support pylons on the left, while Admiral Justman and West took up positions on the right.

The space between the two doors functioned as an airlock in emergency situations. Like the bridge of a starship, the control center was designed to act as a lifeboat. The heavy blast doors were designed to protect both the station and the control center in that event.

The station's fusion reactors powered the shield that provided extra protection for the outer door. It was not nearly as powerful as the exterior shields, but it was holding reasonably well against Klingon hand weapons.

When the shield and then the outer blast door fell, Kirk and the other three officers would defend that outer corridor first. Kirk had no illusions about how long the four of them would hold off the Klingons.

When they had to fall back, they would be falling back into the control room itself. After that, there would be nowhere to go.

Kirk knew that if he had to, if they couldn't defend this room, he would destroy the crystals.

The pounding on the shield outside intensified again. It wouldn't be long.

Kirk flipped open his communicator. "Mr. Spock? Where are you?"

"We're in the station's central hub, but are encountering resistance from the Klingons," Spock said.

Spock's tone of voice was even, though Kirk could hear the sounds of movement—running, actually—in the background. Given what they were facing here, Kirk knew that the resistance the team was facing was serious.

They would not have the station's weapons and shields any time soon—certainly not soon enough to do anything about the Klingons currently at the control room's outer door.

"Captain," Justman called out. Kirk looked at the admiral's position and saw that he was speaking into his communicator.

"The shield is failing," Justman said.

"Understood," Kirk said, and turned his attention back to the blast door.

From the sound of the pounding on the shield, it was amazing that it was holding at all. Kirk barely had time to complete that thought when there was a loud crackle. The sound was unmistakable: the shield had failed.

Immediately, Kirk could hear the sound of disruptor fire striking the blast doors. After a few moments, the doors began to glow in several places.

It will not be long now, he realized.

The Klingons caught Kyle and the group in the last intersection of corridors before they reached the cargo bay. Chief Brantley was leading. As he turned the corner, a Klingon weapon's blast exploded against the bulkhead behind him, barely missing his head and neck.

Brantley ducked for cover as Lieutenant Kyle, Briggs, and Mr. Scott returned fire, pinning the Klingons behind the corner of a bulkhead down a narrow side corridor.

As the phaser came alive in his hand, a sick feeling rose in Kyle's throat. He forced it back down.

Brantley pointed to the door across the intersection that led into the cargo bay, which held the transporter inside. As he kept up the fire, the chief said, "If we get across that open area and inside, the cargo-bay door will hold the Klingons back long enough for us to beam aboard the *Enterprise*."

Scott nodded, but Kyle knew that even if they did get

across and into the cargo bay, there was no guarantee that the transporter would work.

"One at a time," Brantley said. "We make a run for it. Ensign, you and I will cover Mr. Scott and Kyle."

Ensign Briggs nodded.

"We'll get that door open," Mr. Scott said, "and Kyle will come back around the corner to cover you."

Brantley nodded, and Kyle stopped firing as Mr. Scott did. He saw Scott's body tense for the run. The chief engineer seemed ready, though Kyle's own legs felt like lead and his body felt frozen in place.

"It's all right, laddie, just move when I do," Scott said.

Scott's words broke the spell, and Kyle felt like his body was back under his own control. Then Scott stepped to the corner and stood above the crouched Ensign Briggs, who was firing down the hallway at the Klingons trying to work their way toward them.

Incredibly Ensign Briggs's shot tore into the closest Klingon, throwing him backward and—thankfully—out of sight.

The Mr. Scott was moving, and Lieutenant Kyle, head down, followed the chief engineer across the open area, not even drawing a shot as the other Klingons remained behind cover.

"They're going to try to come in around us," Chief Brantley said, pointing down a third hallway.

Kyle saw Scotty nod and knew that they had to move fast to get into that cargo bay. At least there they had a fighting chance. Out here they were in the open and pinned down.

Lieutenant Kyle hit the control panel on the cargo-bay door and it slid open. Mr. Scott headed across the large room at a run. Kyle knew the chief engineer was headed for the transporter but did not even spare a look in that direction.

He immediately turned back and started firing on the Klingons' position. Remarkably, there was no fire from them. Kyle had a bad feeling but stayed focused on his task.

Then Chief Brantley appeared, heading toward him at a run. An instant later, Ensign Briggs was on the chief's heels.

Kyle kept up his fire, though the Klingons did not appear or return fire.

Then Brantley was racing through the door. Briggs was about to do the same when Kyle saw a flash out of the corner of his eye.

Before his mind registered that the Klingons had somehow made their way around to a new position, Kyle saw a second bolt tear into the running Briggs from behind.

The force off the blast lifted the ensign of the ground and threw him against the wall less than a meter from Kyle's position.

He hit with remarkable force and for a moment Kyle was looking straight into the dying man's eyes. Then Briggs was sliding to the floor. Unable to look away, Kyle looked at Briggs as he fell. The damage done by the disruptor was terrible and there was a large portion of his right side that was just not there.

Then a disruptor bolt struck the wall where Briggs's head was just a moment before, and Kyle realized that he had stopped firing.

He felt a hand grab him from behind, and then he was flying backward. As he slid onto the deck, he saw Chief Brantley hitting the control panel from the inside, and the cargo-bay door slammed down.

As Kyle was getting to his feet, Brantley said, "Can you lock the system so it can't be opened from the outside?"

Kyle shook his head. He wanted to tell Brantley about Ensign Briggs, but the chief was shouting something again.

"The door! Do it now!" the chief shouted, shocking Kyle out of his confusion.

Then the lieutenant was racing for the door. He pulled open the control panel. Like most of the equipment, this system was old. It took him a moment to find the right circuit; then he grabbed it and pulled the wire clean out of the panel. The system shorted immediately.

"That will hold them," Kyle said, even as he heard disruptor fire slam against the door.

Kyle caught Brantley's eyes and said, "Sorry, Chief...I—"

"Don't worry about it. You did fine," Brantley said.

Then Kyle was following Brantley to the rear of the cargo bay, where Mr. Scott was at work at the transporter control board. Kyle glanced at the transporter itself. It was an older cargo model and had a single, roughly two-meter-square transporter pad, rather than the individual personal pads.

"Does it work?" Brantley asked Scott.

The chief engineer nodded. "It has power."

Kyle took a quick at the console. "It's not rated for human transport," Kyle said.

"What does that mean?" Brantley asked.

"It does not have the resolution to guarantee one hundred percent accuracy in the rematerialization," Scott said.

The barrage against the bay door increased, and Kyle could see it was glowing in a number of places.

"So it's not *completely* safe," Brantley said, glancing at the door. "*Reasonably* safe is good enough for me."

Scott leaned under the transporter operator's console and pulled open the access door.

"Kyle," Scott said. "I'm going to boost the power to the molecular imaging scanners. Cross-circuit to B."

Kyle performed the operation.

And then Scott was standing next to him.

"Good enough?" Brantley said.

"Yes," Scott said. "The *Enterprise*'s pattern buffer should compensate for any degradation in the signal."

Should? Kyle thought.

"Good enough for me," Brantley said.

"I'll need just a minute to set the transporter to operate on a time delay. Get on the pad," Scott said.

Kyle and Brantley stepped onto the pad. The security section chief seemed incredibly calm. Of course, he did not know what Kyle knew. He did not know how many things could go wrong in the transport—signal decay, quantum shifts, signal-compatibility problems between this outdated system and the *Enterprise*'s newer transporter.

Then Kyle saw the cargo-bay door begin to buckle in a number of places. Holes were showing through. A moment later disruptor bolts tore through them and into the bay, striking cargo containers across the room.

Whatever their chances were on the transporter, they

were better than if they stayed in this room even a few more minutes.

"Powering up," Scott said, racing to take his own position on the transporter pad. But the moment Scott reached the pad, there was a bang and smoke billowed from under the panel.

Mr. Scott raced back to the console and said, "Blew the automatic transport controls." Already, his hands were racing across the console. Kyle saw Brantley's eyes dart between the chief engineer and the rapidly failing door.

Kyle saw in an instant that Mr. Scott would not have time to repair the damage. They had less than a minute, perhaps only seconds.

But they could not fail. Too much was riding on them. Mr. Scott had to get the *Enterprise*'s engines back online. And the others had fought so hard. Ensign Briggs had died to give them this chance.

Kyle knew he had not contributed much to the fight. He was no warrior, he realized, but there was something he could do—a contribution he could make.

"I can run the board, sir," Kyle said, stepping down.

Scott looked up quickly. He obviously knew they were out of time and he understood what Kyle wanted to do.

"Lad..." Scott said.

"We're out of time," Kyle said. "They need you on the *Enterprise*."

Kyle took a step toward the console, but a hand pulled him back.

"This is my job," Chief Brantley said. "Get on the pads, both of you."

"Chief—" Scott said.

"We don't have time. Let me do my job and then you can do yours," Brantley said.

"Aye," Scott said as Brantley stood behind the operator's console.

Mr. Scott grabbed Kyle and pulled him onto the transporter pad.

The lieutenant could see that Brantley looked completely calm as he watched them take their places.

"Don't worry about me," he said. "I have a surprise planned for the Klingons. Just get the *Enterprise* into the fight."

"Aye," Scott said. "Good luck, Chief."

"You too, sir," Brantley said as he pushed forward on the transporter controls.

A moment later Kyle felt the transporter beam take him. In the instant before he was dematerialized he saw the cargo door collapse completely behind the chief.

Chapter Thirteen

FINALLY, Karel thought with satisfaction as the cargo-bay door finally gave way. The Earthers were good at running and hiding. *No doubt from generations of practice in cowardice.*

Well, Klingons had generations of practice in open combat.

Karel was first through the door, his blaster blazing. Among the seventeen Klingons behind him was Gash. Karel was determined to not concern himself with what the large Klingon might do, though with so much disruptor fire in the air it would be easy for Gash to take his own revenge on Karel.

Nevertheless, Karel decided to remain focused on his vengeance and hope that Gash would have the sense to destroy the Empire's enemies first.

He caught a brief flash of energy from the corner of

the room and saw the last moments of the transporter's dematerialization process.

He spat a string of Klingon curses at the cowardly Earthers, who had made running away an art form.

He scanned the empty room and called for the others to halt. "The Earthers have escaped," he said.

"No," said a voice behind him. Karel turned to see Gash searching the room with his one good eye. In that moment Karel knew that he had nothing to worry about from the Klingon, at least until this battle was over. At the moment, Karel could see that Gash was deep in the heat of battle, his blood burning with a desire to crush the Earthers.

"Someone is here," Gash said. "I can smell his Earther stink."

Karel nodded. "Split up. Half on that side," he said, pointing to the left side of the large room. "And half with me," he said, as he headed to the right.

As he walked, he aimed and fired at the transporter console, watching in satisfaction as it went up in a flash of light and energy. *No more Earthers will be escaping from there,* he thought.

When the attack came, it came with surprising swiftness. The large cargo container shot forward, more than a meter off the ground.

"Down," Karel said as he dove to the side. Ignoring the sound of slower warriors getting smashed by the heavy containers, Karel rolled to his feet and fired his disruptor at where he guessed the Earthers had launched the container.

There was no reply and Karel was certain that the

Earthers had hidden themselves somewhere else among the stacks and rows of containers.

"Caution, warriors. They are using antigrav units," Karel said.

He turned to see that two warriors were on the ground. One of them was breathing, but he would not be rejoining the fight, Karel realized.

Two more reasons to crush the Earthers, he thought.

"Show yourselves, Earthers," he called out in their weakling English.

Not surprisingly there was no reply.

He ordered one of his warriors to guard the door in case the Earthers tried to escape that way. There would be no escape for them, not now. This cargo bay would be the Earthers' killing box.

Then he ordered the other warriors to circle the cargo bay so they could trap the Earthers in the middle.

As Karel and his Klingons reached the right side of the bay, he saw movement on the left side. An even larger cargo container, perhaps three meters square, was racing toward three of the warriors there. The Klingons had barely enough time to see the danger before they were crushed between the heavy container and the bulkhead.

He did not have to look to know that the Klingons were dead.

"Arrrggg!" Karel shouted in frustration.

These Earthers would pay for the blood of those warriors. Then phaser fire tore into one of his warriors, forcing the others to dive for cover.

Karel stood his ground and saw movement and a flash

of Starfleet uniform. The Earthers were near the far left-hand corner of the cargo bay, he realized.

"There." Karel pointed. "Get the Earthers!" he shouted.

All the remaining Klingons converged on that point, blasters tearing into bulkheads and cargo containers there.

There was no return fire, but when Karel's Klingons approached, he saw the largest container yet shoot out from against the bulkhead.

Karel's blaster immediately sought out the space where the cargo container had begun moving. To his surprise, there was no one there.

Just as the realization hit him of where the Earthers had gone, phaser fire blasted the two Klingons next to him.

Aiming carefully, Karel blasted the single antigrav unit that was attached to the container's side. The massive object immediately slammed into the ground and a single Earther went flying forward from the top of the container.

The Earther hit the ground hard on one shoulder. Amazingly, he twisted his damaged body quickly and managed to fire at and hit another warrior before half a dozen blaster bolts struck him squarely.

In a flash of light, the Earther was gone.

Still alert, Karel scanned the cargo bay for any more, but his blood told him there were no Earthers there.

It was unbelievable but true. A single, cornered Earther had dealt them a serious blow. Seven Klingon warriors were dead or injured.

His blood rebelled against the idea. It was impossible for the weakling cowards.

His communicator sounded. "What do you want?" he barked into it.

"Make your way to the control room," Koloth's voice said. "The Earthers are resisting strongly. We need to get the crystals and end this now. I will feel better when this station and the *Enterprise* are space debris."

Karel acknowledged the order and ordered his Klingons out of the cargo bay.

Transport seemed instantaneous and smooth to Kyle, but by the look on the transporter operator's face, he could tell that their rematerialization on the *Enterprise* transporter pad had been anything but smooth.

As soon as the transport was complete, Mr. Scott was barreling for the door and Kyle was right on his heels. As they headed for the turbolift, Kyle realized he was still carrying his phaser.

He quickly attached the weapon to his belt and decided that if he never had to fire one again, it would be soon enough.

Moments later they were exiting the turbolift at a run.

The engineering section of the *Enterprise* had never looked so good as far as Lieutenant Kyle was concerned. He had been convinced they weren't going to make it. Surprisingly, his biggest concern had been that Briggs's sacrifice would have been in vain.

And Brantley's.

Though the section chief seemed confident, Kyle knew the chances of a single person against a large Klingon attack force were not good. Nevertheless, he was certain that Brantley had given them a surprise or two.

Now came the really tricky part. They had to cold-start a starship warp core.

But Mr. Scott had done it once and Spock had refined the formula since then. It would be difficult, but Kyle was relieved to have a task in front of him that he had confidence he could do. He would be able to make a contribution.

Kyle remembered what had happened the last time the *Enterprise* had done this. It wasn't something he wanted to go through again. Yet Mr. Scott had assured him the new formula didn't have the same problems.

"It'll work, laddie," Mr. Scott had said.

The statement hadn't reassured him much. But he did believe completely in Mr. Scott and his ability to work miracles. Kyle just hoped this wasn't going to be the time Mr. Scott couldn't pull that rabbit out of the engineering hat.

Mr. Scott fired orders as he strode into the engine room. Men scrambled to stations, following his commands instantly.

"We're goin' to cold-start this darlin'," he said to everyone in the control room. "Stand ready now."

Scott took up his post at the main engineering control board. "And we're goin' to do it in record time."

Kyle marveled at the speed of Mr. Scott's fingers as they danced over the controls. Every so often he'd shout an order, but most of the time he worked the board like a master artist, never seeming to hesitate, never missing a beat.

Kyle knew that even under the best of conditions, cold-starting a warp core would take some time. Not as much as a slow warm-up did—not nearly. But it still took time. And with the Klingons overrunning the station, time was in short supply.

After the first minute of watching Mr. Scott, Kyle started to actually believe Scott might pull this off, if the Klingons gave them enough time.

After two minutes of watching, Kyle was convinced.

"Mr. Kyle," Scott said as he worked the control board. "I want you to wait for my signal and download the new intermix data to the dilithium chamber. I have rerouted to use all available backup circuits. Make sure they hold."

"Yes, sir," Kyle said as he took the board. He spared a glance at the chief engineer as he headed out toward the Jefferies tube.

"Mr. Scott and Lieutenant Kyle are on board, sir," acting Communications Officer Perez said.

"Good," Uhura said. She wouldn't bother Mr. Scott just yet. He would have his hands full with the engines.

"Status of the Klingon ship?" she said. "Did they react to the transport?"

"No," the acting science officer said. "They are maintaining a weapons lock on us, but have not moved their position."

Good, Uhura thought. *Maybe Scotty will have the time he needs to make a difference.*

Around her the crew sat silent, watching the screen, waiting for something to happen. There wasn't a thing they could do, and that felt odd to her. It felt wrong.

This was a crew that was used to action, yet right now all the action was taking place on the starbase. The *En-*

terprise was—for the moment—nearly powerless and playing dead so that the Klingons wouldn't move against her.

Uhura hated the feeling of nothing to do. She always had. And now she resisted trying to come up with something to help. The captain's plan was a good one, and her job was to wait until the engines were powered so that the *Enterprise* could strike when the Klingons weren't expecting it.

So she had to sit, wait, and just watch.

Kirk knew his enemy well enough to know they wouldn't bother firing on the *Enterprise* if the *Enterprise* appeared dead in space.

"The fighting near the station's control area has intensified," the acting science officer said. "And also near the engineering decks."

Uhura nodded. "Stay ready, Mr. Sulu. I want to be able to move the minute Mr. Scott gets the engines powered back up."

"Understood," Sulu said, nodding.

Around her the bridge went back to deep, uncomfortable silence. The silence of watching and waiting and worrying, with nothing to do.

Chapter Fourteen

KELL AND THE REST of the squad met no resistance down the long corridor as they raced toward the center of the station.

Finally, they crossed the last blast-door frame, which separated the central hub from the perpendicular spoke they had been traversing.

Kell could see that the fighting in the hub had been intense. There was angry scoring everywhere and a lot of blasted equipment and walls that had obviously taken direct disruptor and phaser fire.

As they crossed the threshold to the central hub, they could hear both phaser and disruptor fire. Remaining on their course to the center of the station, they passed circular corridor after corridor that ringed the central hub.

At what Kell estimated must be the midway point,

Kell and the others saw a Starfleet security force come running down one of the curved corridors.

There were four security officers, and another officer, a lieutenant, that was wearing command gold.

They stopped when they saw Kell's team, and the lieutenant conferred with Fuller.

"Heavy fighting, the Klingons have control of that sector," he said, pointing behind him.

"We're pulling back to the outer sector," he said. "I suggest you do the same."

Then the lieutenant and his team were running down the corridor that Kell and his group had just come down.

"We have no choice," Fuller said. "We have to get to the warp core."

Fuller led the charge and the squad followed. They passed corridor after corridor, and the sounds of fighting became louder and more intense.

The station was fighting for its life. And from the ratio of disruptor to phaser blasts that he heard, Kell could see the station was losing.

Finally, they came to a central bank of turbolifts. Fuller and Spock tried one after the other and found that none of the turbolift doors would open.

Finally, Jawer called out, "I found the emergency turbolift, sir."

Kell ran up behind him and could see that the turbolift was marked in red, ENGINEERING, FOR EMERGENCIES ONLY.

The doors were closed, but Jawer had the control panel open and was doing something inside.

There was a flash of sparks and Jawer pulled his hand back. Then he looked expectantly at the turbolift doors.

Obediently, they opened, and Jawer started inside. Kell sensed the danger before he saw it. His hand reached out automatically and grabbed Jawer by the uniform, pulling him back.

Then he looked into the shaft and saw that there was no car there, just the shaft. Kell peered over the edge and saw that it was a long way down.

Jawer gave him an embarrassed grin and said, "Um, thanks."

Fuller surveyed the lift and cursed under his breath. "Okay, it looks like we do this the hard way. Head for the stairs."

Before he was finished issuing the order, Fuller was heading for the door about twenty meters away that read EMERGENCY STAIRS.

When the Klingons came through the breach in the door, they came through as a wall of bodies, firing their deadly disruptors in all directions as they shouted out some sort of battle cry.

Kirk and the others returned fire.

From their covered positions, the Starfleet officers were able to strike with deadly accuracy. The captain picked one target, then another. He did not wait to see if his beams struck. He simply moved to another target in the mass of Klingon bodies that were charging them.

Whatever deficiencies the Klingons might have, Kirk realized, courage was not one of them. Their losses were astonishingly high.

In the first minute of the battle, the Klingons lost at least four times the number of the four Starfleet defenders.

And the charge was remarkably effective, with the lead Klingons reaching less than two meters from their position before they fell.

Finally, the advance stopped and there were more than a dozen Klingon bodies in the few meters in front of the Starfleet men.

Then new fire erupted from a covered position that was just outside the frame of the ruined outer door.

As a beam tore incredibly close to him, Kirk realized that a few of the warriors had found positions inside the outer door. Kirk shook his head in amazement.

The Klingons had sacrificed a large number of their group to get better firing positions on the Starfleet people.

We don't have long, Kirk realized.

Even if the disruptor blasts didn't find them soon, Kirk did not doubt that the main Klingon force would make another charge to get more Klingons into position.

"Pull back, Captain," Justman's voice called out. "We'll cover you."

"Let's go," Kirk said to the base security guard next to him. "I'll head for the control panel, you get inside and provide cover as quickly as you can."

Then Kirk was up and running, firing the phaser behind him as he moved.

Staying the phaser, he hit the control panel, which opened the door. Turning around again, he fired his phaser as disruptor bolts tore around him. Kirk saw the base security officer dash for the door...and catch a disruptor bolt directly in the back.

He went flying into the control room and Kirk did not have to check to see that the man was dead.

Twisting his body, Kirk was inside the door and firing from the cover of the doorframe. "Now, Admiral!" he shouted.

Justman and West moved together, sprinting out from their cover and straight into the open door.

As soon as they were inside, Kirk hit the switch and the heavy door slammed down from above, cutting off the stray disruptor fire that was shooting into the control room.

He looked at the ensign's body on the floor. The wound was terrible, so wide that you could see the deck through it. Kirk held his gaze on the young man for a moment and realized that he had never even learned the security officer's name.

Looking up, he took in the rest of the room. Ensign Marsilii had opened one of the control panels and was furiously working inside. The four base lieutenants were at their stations looking to Admiral Justman and to him for an answer.

They all knew how long it had taken for the Klingons to penetrate the outer door, and, thus, how long they had before the control room became a battleground.

Kirk knew they would all fight and fight well, but he also knew they would not last long against the kind of force they had faced outside.

His communicator beeped and he flipped it open. "Kirk here," he said.

"Captain," Uhura's voice said. "Mr. Scott is on board the *Enterprise*."

Relief washed over him. It was small progress, but it was progress and they had suffered nothing but setbacks so far. And Kirk had not yet heard from Mr. Spock, and that worried him.

"Let me know when the engines are starting up. Kirk out," he said.

A look at the door told Kirk that whatever miracle Scotty worked on the *Enterprise,* it would not happen in time to help them here.

"The *Enterprise* will be back online in just a few minutes," Kirk said to the admiral.

"We don't have that long," Justman said.

Kirk knew it was true. They had minutes before the Klingons came through the door.

"Should we destroy the crystals, then?" Kirk said, pointing to the two cargo containers.

The admiral shook his head decisively. "Not yet, Captain. I propose something else. We just need to slow them down to give Mr. Spock some time to get to the station's warp core."

Kirk glanced at the admiral as a loud explosion rattled the control room and shook the door. Obviously, the Klingons had found something else to throw against the door.

And by the gleam in the admiral's eye and the slight grin on his face, it was clear the admiral had a plan.

He turned to one of the control-room crew, a young lieutenant manning the science station. "Ensign, will that door lead us out of the control-room area?" he said, pointing to the access door that they had taken to get inside after docking the travel pod to the station.

"Yes, sir," the young man said. "There is a small airlock that leads to a small access corridor that follows the main corridor."

Kirk followed the lieutenant's pointing finger with his eyes. The door that had led them into the control room was to the right of the main viewscreen; a team would have to make their way in the small space between the inner and outer shells of the control room, then to the access corridor. Presumably, there would be access to the main corridor a short distance away.

Kirk could see what the admiral was planning. "A small team could lead some or all of the Klingon force away," he said.

"Exactly," Justman replied. Then the admiral turned to West and said, "How would the Klingons likely respond to a hard hit to their flank?"

Without blinking, West said, "Strongly. They would regard the attack as an insult and pursue."

Kirk was impressed. "Request permission to lead the team," he said.

"No, Captain. I will do that," Justman replied.

"But, Admiral—" Kirk began.

"You will stay here and guard the crystals," Justman said. Then, before Kirk could voice his protest, he said, "That's an order, Captain."

"I would like to come with you, Admiral," West said.

Justman nodded and said, "The two of us should be sufficient for the task. Our goal is not to defeat them, just to lead them away and give you more time in here."

Then he gave Kirk a smile. "I know what you can do, Captain. That's why I want you in here. Starfleet needs those crystals."

"The chance you'll be taking," Kirk said, "is getting

trapped between two groups of Klingons in the main corridor."

"Perhaps, but I still have a few maneuvers left in me," Justman said.

"Which direction will you go?"

"Anywhere away from this area," the admiral said. "Even if I draw away just half of the ones out there, it will give you a better chance of holding out in here."

With a nod, Admiral Justman nodded and ducked through the door, his weapon ready, followed quickly by Lieutenant West.

A few moments later the sound of disruptor fire intensified against the door, which was glowing red in a number of places.

Kirk turned to the control-center crew, who were now all looking to him. He gave them a grim smile. He was not out of maneuvers either.

"Mr. Marsilii," he said. "Are you ready?"

"Just about," the young man replied, closing up the control panel.

After he ran his hands over the panel to test the circuits, Marsilii pointed to a green switch on the console.

"That will initiate an emergency plasma venting from all of the shield emitters." Marsilii shrugged apologetically. "I couldn't restrict the venting to the emitter nearest the Klingon ship."

"That's fine, Ensign. You've given us the first real weapon of this fight."

Lieutenant West and Admiral Justman made their way around the narrow walkway that circled the control room. At the point nearly opposite the door they had used to access this area, they found a small airlock door.

The admiral used his command codes and the airlock swung open. Then they spent a few meters in the airlock's even smaller corridor, finally coming to another airlock door.

The admiral used his command codes again and then they were inside yet another service corridor, one that his internal compass told him ran parallel to the main corridor.

A few hundred meters later, there was a service door that West knew would take them into the main corridor.

The admiral didn't waste any time. He hit the control panel and jumped into the corridor. West followed him at a run. Fifty meters later, they were in firing range behind what looked like a large Klingon force that was firing at the control center door. They were moving some kind of heavy equipment into place.

The two men took positions at an intersecting corridor, taking cover there.

Again, the admiral did not hesitate. He said, "Target their equipment first and fire when I do."

West understood. Even in this dire situation, Justman would not shoot the Klingons in the back.

Justman fired, and West's beam lanced out a moment later.

The heavy equipment went up in a single large, explosive blast, tossing Klingons in each direction. Whatever it was that they had hit, West was glad that the Klingons had not had the chance to use it against the control room.

The two Starfleet officers kept up the fire until the Klingons regrouped and turned to them. The disruptor fire came a moment later, but Justman held his position until the Klingon force started to move forward.

West understood and kept up fire. Then inspiration struck him and he called out, using some of the few Klingon words he had learned, "Bloodless cowards!"

The words had an immediate effect, and the Klingons started after them at a dead run.

Shots exploding against the station wall behind him, Admiral Justman fired one last shot at the Klingons chasing them. Then he turned to run. West followed him down the corridor, glad for the moment that they had a few seconds before the Klingons would be able to make the turn and start firing again. For the moment, they had a good running head start.

So far, the plan had worked.

"Do you know where this hallway leads?" West asked.

"No," Admiral Justman said as he continued.

Then they followed a turn in the corridor and West saw that it led straight into a dead end.

No, not quite a dead end. There was a large door that had a sign over it that read, ARBORETUM.

They reached the door just as the first disruptor blasts tore at the walls and floor around them.

Then, a moment later, they were inside a huge structure that was full of rows of plants, everything from tables with potted plants to large trees.

Above them was a large clear dome. West could see the *Enterprise* hanging in space. And the planet beyond it.

Chapter Fifteen

KELL WATCHED FROM ABOVE as Fuller stepped through the open doors and out into the corridor.

Right behind him, Kell came out firing in the opposite direction. Kell's side was clear, though he heard the chief fire his phaser and turned to see a Klingon warrior fall. Even as his mind was counting the small Klingon force, his hand was firing.

Fuller, Kell, and the rest of the security team who were filing out of the emergency stairway were out in the open. The five Klingons were as well, but the security squad had the advantage of surprise.

The five warriors fell quickly and the team dashed down the corridor to the next flight of emergency stairs. The stairs for each level were not directly above one another. There were staggered by about fifty meters, so that damage to one stairwell would not affect them all.

As they made their way down farther and farther, they had found fewer and fewer of the Klingon borders. Kell hoped this was a good sign—a sign that the Klingons had not yet made their way to engineering.

Kell knew they had lost a lot of time on the stairs, descending nearly thirty decks to reach the warp core. If they lost much more time, the station and the crystals might already be lost.

He hoped that Kirk was faring well. He remembered being knocked to the ground by Orion fire in the caves of the second planet in System 1324. He had opened his eyes to see Kirk seeming to rise out of the smoke. The captain was holding his phaser rifle, looking like an ancient Klingon warrior wielding a *bat'leth* and ready to fight a great serpent.

Kell decided that Kirk would succeed. And there was the admiral as well. Kell had seen what ensigns and lieutenants in Starfleet could accomplish. He could only imagine what it might be like to watch an admiral in action.

Down another stairwell and out into another corridor. This one was clear.

Then another. Then another.

"Five more levels," the Vulcan announced.

Each of the five levels was clear. Then they came to the blast doors that were the only entrance to the engineering levels and the warp core.

Fuller entered the engineering deck first, with the others immediately behind him. Kell was amazed by the scale of the warp core, many times larger than any core on a ship he had ever seen.

It shot up at least ten decks in each direction. It was

ringed by at least five engineering decks full of bank after bank of computers and other equipment. Each deck looked over the warp core and had a short guardrail.

A quick scan told Kell that there were no Klingons in the area and the engineering staff was dead.

Parrish was by his side. She surveyed the dead on the ground, at least twenty of them.

"Monsters," she said. She was referring to the Klingons who had done this, beings of his blood. He wondered what she would think if and when she ever learned about his true face.

Suddenly Kell understood why they had met no Klingon boarders here. After the other Infiltrator that Port mentioned shut off the core, Klingon warriors had obviously come and killed the engineers. The Klingons had not bothered to secure the decks because the warp core should take hours to restart and the Klingons expected the battle to be long over by then. They believed there was no threat here.

Spock went immediately to a console that overlooked the core. Jawer was at his side.

"How much time do you need?" Chief Fuller asked.

"No more than thirty minutes," Spock said, his voice even.

"Chief," a voice called.

Kell turned to see Parrish's new partner, Ensign Clancy, at a security console nearby. Fuller rushed over and the others followed, leaving Spock and Jawer to their work.

"We tripped some sort of alarm when we entered," Clancy said.

"Standard station security?" Kell asked.

"That is what I thought until I saw this," Clancy said, pointing at a cutaway view of this sector of the station on the viewscreen. A large red dot was making its way down toward their level.

"Klingons," Clancy said. "A lot of them and they know we are here."

"How many ways are there into this area?" Fuller asked.

"Just this door," Clancy said.

That made sense. In the event that the warp core needed to be jettisoned in an emergency, there would only be a single door to close to protect the rest of the station from the vacuum of space.

"Can you set the door to lock from the inside?" Fuller asked.

Clancy ran her hands over the panel and said, "Yes. Just hit this button and no one on the other side will be able to get through without blasting the door down."

Fuller studied the station schematics for a moment. They looked like gibberish to Kell, but the chief seemed to be able to make sense of them.

Spock appeared behind them.

Fuller turned and said, "Mr. Spock, hit this switch when we leave. We will hold the Klingons off as long as we can. If they get past us, the door will offer you some more protection—but it might just be minutes."

"Understood. Thank you, Chief," the Vulcan said.

"Let's move," Fuller said, racing for the door.

Through the clear dome West could see part of the planet's surface drifting slowly past and the dark starfield beyond it. Under normal circumstances, this view would have stopped even the hardest of nature critics. A beautiful planetscape, large green trees, a small lake bordered by flowers. This old and very well tended arboretum was magnificent.

The smell of all the flowers and plants formed a thick backdrop to the fight, as the smell of phaser fire added to the mix.

And the dark emergency lighting combined with the natural light reflected from the planet gave everything a bluish tint.

With the Klingons behind them, this arboretum wasn't a place West really wanted to be right now, or a place he would have chosen to make a stand. There was too much open space, too many ways for the Klingons to flank them. Especially with just Admiral Justman and himself.

Then Klingons began coming through the door.

And there were a lot more Klingons. Somehow, along the way, the force chasing them had gotten bigger. Admiral Justman figured that the original ones had been joined by others who had been on the way to the control room. West knew they had killed or incapacitated some when they struck their heavy equipment, but these Klingons just kept coming. The entire Klingon battle cruiser must almost be empty by now.

"We can't let them take us here," Admiral Justman said, sticking his head out quickly to see around the tree trunk.

"I agree," West said. "If they take us here, the Klingons will have quick access back to the control-room area. We're the only thing between them, Captain Kirk, and those crystals."

But there was only one way in or out. And for the moment, the Klingons were using it as an entrance.

From what West could figure, there wasn't an option left open to them except to simply hold out as long as they could.

Justman ducked out from behind the tree, fired, and then got back into cover as three return shots pounded their position, one breaking off a limb over their heads. For a moment, West wondered if the legendary Admiral Justman was out of miracles.

"I still have a few maneuvers left," Admiral Justman said, once again, seeming to read West's mind.

"Of course, sir," West said, firing at the Klingons as they came through the door. Between them, Justman and West were hitting a good number of the warriors, but for every three they hit, another made it inside the arboretum.

"We don't have to beat them. We're still buying time," Justman said.

"Spock hasn't made it to the warp core yet," West said.

"We don't know that," Justman said. "But I think it's about time we get an update, don't you?" He pulled out his communicator and clicked it open as West made sure the Klingons weren't moving up on them too quickly.

"Admiral Justman to Captain Kirk."

"Glad to hear your voice, Admiral," Kirk said, loud enough for West to hear from his place. "Where are you?"

"Pinned down in the arboretum, holding off a Klingon force. How about you?"

"They are still outside," Kirk said. "You bought us the time. The door is holding."

"I'm glad to hear that, Captain," Justman said.

"Scott reports progress on the *Enterprise*," Kirk said. "And Spock is at the warp core now."

"Excellent, Captain," Justman said. "This will be a game of inches and of seconds from here on. We'll slow them down here as long as we can."

"Thank you, Admiral," Kirk said.

Justman closed the communicator and tucked it away. "Looks like we have to buy more time. Let's head back toward those trees and boxes near the edge. That position looks easier to defend."

"I'll cover you," West said.

"No, better we both go together," Justman said. "More chance one of us will make it."

West nodded. It had occurred to him that he might die at any minute but he had not considered the possibility of the admiral not making it. Admiral Justman—the hero of Donatu V—certainly he could not be stopped by Klingon fire from a hand disruptor.

"Now," Justman said.

Both he and Justman fired off covering shots from their phasers, then turned and ran, trying to keep the tree they had been behind between them and the Klingons.

It took at least ten running steps for the Klingons to see what they were doing. It was too long, and the volley of return fire from the Klingons missed them as they dove for cover behind a group of oaklike trees and what looked like metal alien plant-growth chambers.

Incredibly, after a few minutes the Klingon fire stopped. West realized they must have gotten them all. For now, anyway.

Justman glanced at West. "I think we just bought a few more minutes. Now let them they try to find us."

West nodded. Then he waited. This lull in the battle would last seconds, no more, he knew. Then the Klingon fire would rain around them again. He was prepared to answer it, and prepared to make the Klingons pay for every step they took farther into the station.

"Start destroying those control panels," Kirk shouted to the five young starbase officers still in the command center. From the sound of the disruptor fire against the door, the admiral had succeeded in drawing off half or more of the Klingons at the door.

Yet the ones who remained kept at their task. That task was taking longer than it would have with more weapons at work, but Kirk knew it would end the same way.

And it would end very quickly.

The admiral's plan had been a good one. It had bought them some time. Kirk regretted that it would not be enough.

The Klingons would be storming the room and would soon overrun them. The first job was to make sure that the weapons and other controls were not available to the Klingons. That way, when Spock succeeded and got the warp core back online, the Klingons would not be able to use the station's weapons against the *Enterprise*.

It occurred to the captain that he had no doubt that Spock would succeed. He only hoped he lived to congratulate the Vulcan and recommend another commendation for him.

Normally, Kirk would have been satisfied to use command codes to lock them out of the station's computer, but there had been too many security breaches. Destroying the controls and interfaces was the only way to be sure.

Methodically, the crew destroyed the consoles that controlled weapons and shields, even the computer interface panel—anything that could be used as a weapon by the attackers. The only systems they left intact were sensors and the viewscreen so that Kirk could monitor the Klingons until the last second.

And, of course, Kirk made sure that nothing they destroyed would affect their ability to strike at the Klingon warship with their jury-rigged EM blast. Kirk liked hitting the Klingons with the weapon that the Orions had used against the *Enterprise* when the Orions were working for the Klingons. But that would be a weapon of last resort.

There was no telling what the Klingons would do once they were attacked, and there was no way to know how much the weapon would affect the Klingon ship. They might very well turn around and start blasting the *Enterprise* and the station.

And until the ship and station were back online, Kirk did not want to take that chance.

Smoke poured out of a half-dozen panels, and the air smelled of death and burning wires. Never, even in Kirk's worst nightmares, had he imagined a pitched fight like this for a control room.

The dilithium crystals placed carefully in the cargo containers in the corner troubled him the most. He did not want to destroy them. To do so would waste the admiral's great effort.

Yet there was no hiding them. And even if they evacuated the control room through the access door, he could not trust that they would be able to elude the Klingons for long.

"Prepare to evacuate," he said to the assembled group. "Use the access door and take the corridor as far down as you can."

Then he turned to the young ensign who had rigged the weapon for him. "Mr. Marsilii, please stay with me."

"Yes, sir," he replied.

The others seemed frozen in place.

"What about you, sir?" the acting science officer asked.

"We will be right behind you," Kirk replied.

No one moved.

"That's an order," he said, raising his eyebrows.

The four young lieutenants headed for the access door. "Stay together and avoid contact with the Klingons. You have all done well and you have all done your parts."

The one in the lead opened the door and stepped inside, and the others followed.

Kirk stared at the door. He judged they didn't have much time, just a few minutes now.

He raised his phaser and adjusted it as he walked over to the dilithium cargo containers.

Pausing for just a moment, Captain Kirk raised his phaser, took aim, and then stayed his firing hand.

Something had caught his eye. The food server that was just a few meters away from the cargo containers.

It would work, he was suddenly sure. But if he did it, he would be betting that Scott would have the *Enter-*

prise's warp engines online, that Spock would have the station's core online, and that the still damaged *Enterprise* and the station's relatively low-powered weapons systems would be able to defeat the fully operational and very deadly Klingon battle cruiser.

It would be a big risk and a large bet whose stakes might be the fate of the Federation itself.

Kirk decided to take the bet.

"Ensign Marsilii," he called.

Kirk waited until the young officer was close, then pointed at the food server unit in a small alcove on one side of the control center. "If I'm correct," Kirk said, "the food servers are a form of turbolift, similar to old-style dumbwaiters."

"Yes, sir," Marsilii said. "The system runs throughout the station."

"Will it function on battery power?" Kirk said.

The ensign walked over to the unit and hit the control. It opened.

"Yes, sir," he said. "The system does not require a lot of power and it's on a separate circuit from the personnel turbolifts. I guess the Klingons did not think of knocking out this system."

"Can you program it to go anywhere in the station?" Kirk asked.

Marsilii surveyed the now destroyed environmental control console and shook his head. "No, sir." He worked the simple controls for a moment. "All I can do is a simple program to send the lifts to waste disposal."

"Perfect," said Kirk. "Do it."

"Sir?" Marsilii said as Kirk opened up the lid of the

upper cargo container. Then Marsilii's eyes lit up with understanding. "I get it. A hiding place, sir," he said.

"Yes," Kirk said as he picked up two of the crystals. Even uncut, the large starship-grade crystals were beautiful.

"Will they be safe in the disposal area?" Kirk asked.

"Yes, sir," Marsilii said. "It's just storage. They will likely just pile up with the other waste for reprocessing."

The young ensign worked quickly, but Kirk saw the outer door start to buckle in two places.

"Ensign," Kirk said with an edge to his voice.

"Got it, sir," Marsilii said, turning to the captain.

Kirk smiled and said, "Let's do it," as he lobbed the first crystal to the security officer. He quickly grabbed another from the container and tossed it.

Though the young man had almost certainly never seen starship-grade crystals that closely, he did not hesitate and put the crystal into the server, holding the door open with one hand.

"We can fit two at a time," Marsilii said, catching the second crystal that Kirk tossed.

He let the server door shut and then caught another crystal. A few seconds later the door to the lift opened again. Then he repeated the procedure with another crystal and sent them both on their way.

Working as fast as they could, the two men emptied the crystals into the station's maintenance area while the door continued to buckle. Kirk kept an eye on the entrance and saw the disruptor fire cut two small holes in the door.

Almost immediately, disruptor fire came through the

holes, but the angle was bad and the energy bursts slammed harmlessly into the ceiling.

Finally, the first container was empty and Kirk tossed it aside, taking just a second to blast it with his phaser. He did not disintegrate the storage unit, merely blasted it into pieces. Let the Klingons think they had destroyed the crystals.

It might buy them a little more time.

Kirk opened the second container and tossed Marsilii another crystal. The server door opened and the young man tossed the crystal inside.

Time.

The pounding on the door told him they didn't have much, but at least it was a race.

Chapter Sixteen

ADMIRAL JUSTMAN WAITED, the young Lieutenant West beside him. Justman gripped the phaser tightly in one hand, watching the door. The only thing that stood between the Klingon force and the only remaining entrance to the control center was Justman himself and West.

It had been years since Justman had fired a phaser at another living being. It had happened a handful of times in his long career and the admiral remembered each one with a painful clarity.

Each of those experiences had visited him in his dreams many times in the years since he had moved to Command headquarters and out of active duty on the front lines of Starfleet's exploration and other duties.

Justman knew that many young cadets were extremely proud of their performance in weapons training.

He also knew that their pride in prowess with a phaser lasted only until they used one against another being.

The lucky ones never drew their weapons and never knew what it cost to fight a battle, even if you won. Justman knew the cost too well, but he steeled his resolve. He had watched men and women make greater sacrifices than this unpleasant duty.

When Justman was a young officer—a period that ended at the Battle of Donatu V—he thought he would live to see the galaxy become safer within his lifetime. Like West when he was still at the Academy, Justman thought that Starfleet's greatest victory would be in the battle and wars it prevented through friendship and exchange with other races.

The admiral still believed firmly in that mission and in the possibility that it would succeed one day. But first, he realized, the Federation would have to survive past whatever happened today and in the months that followed. It would have to survive past this crisis with the Klingons.

He was no longer young enough or arrogant enough to think that their success was a given. And he knew that much depended on the outcome of today.

The sound of West's breathing brought him out of his thoughts. The men were crouched behind a low table that contained, according to the placard, a rare flowering hibiscus from Rigel VII. The plant was in bloom and had a sharp but pleasant scent.

He knew it had been moved here and nurtured by Starfleet and Federation personnel who would spend their lives preserving botanical oddities from around the galaxy. He wondered what Klingons would think of that vocation.

From what he had seen of Klingon values, he doubted they would agree with that sort of allocation of resources. But Justman agreed with it, with every fiber of his being. He thought it was a noble calling, as noble as the calling of an army of Starfleet and Federation scientists, anthropologists, doctors, and researchers who were searching the galaxy to learn its secrets.

What would happen to them and to those secrets if they failed in their mission today? He was afraid he knew. Most of those explorers would be dead and much of what they sought would be destroyed as the Klingons conquered the Federation.

Then the Klingons would seek out new worlds, worlds yet unexplored by the Federation. But they would not come to learn, the Klingons would come to conquer, and Justman believed that if they could succeed in the Federation there were few worlds or bodies that would be able to stand against them.

The Klingons, he knew, were powerful. And they understood sacrifice—they had been willing to sacrifice a world of their own kind to continue the fight against the Federation.

Yet he also knew the Klingons could be beaten. He had seen Klingon battle cruisers fall and had known in his heart that he and the Starfleet ships could have won the day over Donatu V. Yet he and the other surviving officers had not been prepared to pay the cost of that victory.

He vowed that he would never make that mistake again.

In a fraction of a second, the doors to the arboretum opened and the Klingons began flooding in. To Justman, they seemed like a swarm.

Their uniforms had changed in twenty-five years, but he saw the same deadly determination on the faces of the warriors who came barreling through the door.

Justman picked his first target and fired, hitting a Klingon directly in the chest. A split second before his beam found its mark, he realized that Lieutenant West had fired and struck another warrior.

The admiral had served with West's father and had seen the young man's record. West had succeeded in virtually every subject and area of training. The admiral believed that West would excel in any area to which he directed his energies.

In a gentler galaxy, West would have built a career as a scientist, a xenoanthropologist, making discoveries on a starship. But instead, Justman had called him into service and brought him to this place.

West found two more targets and Justman found another. The admiral did not have to look at the lieutenant to know that all of his energies and resources were now focused on the fight.

Justman was saddened that this was so, but he saw that West was excelling in this new task. He was sorry to see the last shreds of the young man's innocence being burned away. On the other hand, he was glad to be fighting this fight with the lieutenant.

The Klingons were suffering heavy losses—staggering losses. Yet they kept coming. And a few had escaped Justman's and West's phasers and had found covered positions from which to return fire.

A disruptor bolt struck a display nearby, exploding it with remarkable force.

They have improved those things, Justman noted professionally.

Without discussion, Justman concentrated on returning the Klingon fire while West brought down Klingons as they came through the door. Justman's peripheral vision told him that West was doing it with astonishing accuracy.

Yet a few more made it through.

Justman brought down one more in the first position, leaving two. Then his peripheral vision told him that two more had found cover about ten meters to the right. A moment later, the first blaster bolt rocked the floor nearby.

Justman and West were now in the crossfire of the Klingons in the two positions. Justman alternated his fire between the two positions as West concentrated his fire on the door.

Yet one more got through. Then another.

The disruptor bolts came closer and closer, one hitting the display directly in front of them, throwing up shrapnel and dirt.

Still, the men kept up their fire.

Justman hit a Klingon directly in the chest, then struck another in the shoulder. Justman was not sure if the warrior was dead but the Klingon fell out of sight and there was one less origin point for the disruptor fire.

But another replaced the Klingon quickly.

Another bolt struck very close to Justman and West's position. Justman's peripheral vision told him that two more Klingons were setting up a third, covered firing position.

If the Starfleet men stayed much longer, they would quickly fall to the three-way crossfire. Yet if they pulled

back the door they would be unprotected and the Klingons would soon flood the arboretum.

Admiral Justman did not need his advanced military
training to know that he and West were not fighting a
battle they could win. The best they could do was delay
the inevitable for as long as possible and hope that
bought Kirk and his team enough time to make a difference.

Justman had seen many officers who had made a difference in his career. Too often that difference had required great sacrifice from great men and women.
Suddenly, he saw Captain Rodriguez's face as it looked
twenty-five years ago as clearly as he saw the young man
beside him. He remembered the captain's face before the
disruptor blast from a Klingon warship had blasted the
entire bridge crew out into the cold void of space.

As he got older, Justman found the distance between
the past and the present shrinking, as the distance between two points shrank in the subspace world of warp
dynamics. While the battle raged around him, he could
feel the past and present beginning to fold over one another, forming a continuum.

As he had done many times in his career, Justman
said a short prayer to God and to Captain Rodriguez for
strength.

"Pull back!" he shouted to West.

The young man complied immediately, even though
he knew what the order meant. Then the admiral and the
lieutenant slowly crawled backward with disruptor fire
raining above and all around them now.

When they were a few meters behind the display, Justman shot West a look and rolled across the aisle between the row of displays they were in and the next. As he rolled, the admiral fired toward the Klingons with his phaser.

Then Justman covered West as the young man executed the same maneuver. The admiral noted that West struck at least one of his targets as he rolled and fired. Then the lieutenant was beside him, firing his weapon.

An instant later, the display case that had been their only cover and the rare Rigellian plant it supported exploded under a torrent of blaster fire.

"Back," Justman said, gesturing behind them.

The new angle of fire gave them additional cover, Justman knew, since it put more displays and equipment between the two forces. But that cover wouldn't last long as the Klingons changed their own positions to compensate.

They had to pull back again, then again.

The door that would give the Klingons access to the control room was just twenty meters behind them now. And the Klingons were moving ahead faster as their numbers grew.

It would soon become a game of inches, and seconds, Justman knew.

He racked his brain for some way to add a few seconds to the inevitable, to give Kirk time to pull out a miracle.

He scanned the area around him.

They had moved in a diagonal line toward the door. Above the door and the wall was the beginning of the transparent dome. Just ahead of the door were some compartments that were marked HIGH OXYGEN ENVIRONMENT.

There would be nothing he could use in there. Though he might be able to get one or more of those compartments to explode, the blasts would do little good unless the Klingons cooperated and lined up right in front of them.

Then an idea struck him.

"Cease fire and follow me," Justman said.

The admiral rolled to the next aisle and then the next. Now there were just six or seven meters of open space between them and the arboretum wall.

The admiral stood and ran, motioning West to follow.

He knew he had less than a minute before the Klingons moved far enough ahead to see them, so he acted quickly.

Justman stopped in front of the transparent door he had spied a moment ago. A quick look inside confirmed what the admiral had suspected. Beyond the transparent door, there was a small compartment, then another transparent door that protected the exotic plants that needed the oxygen-rich environment.

The space between the two doors was an airlock that the botanists would use to protect the plants from the low-oxygen environment outside.

"What can I do, Admiral?" West asked.

Justman smiled at the young man. "Patrick, you have done very well today. I want you to know that your father would be very proud of you."

Then in practically one motion, he hit the control panel next to the door with one hand and grabbed West by the shoulder with the other. As the door slid open, he shoved Lieutenant West inside and resealed the door.

Using his phaser, Justman fired at the control panel, sealing the door and the lieutenant outside.

On the other side, West looked at him with confusion, then understanding.

As Justman turned, he heard West pounding on the door from the inside.

The admiral was amazed by his calm as he stepped out for a better firing position. He moved quickly now, taking aim at the support pylon that connected the wall in front of him with the transparent dome above.

The pylon flared out of existence and Justman could immediately hear the hiss of escaping air. Moving quickly, he aimed twenty meters farther down and disintegrated another pylon, then another.

For a moment the only sounds he could hear were the hiss of escaping air—which was strong enough to create a breeze in the arboretum—and Lieutenant West's pounding. Justman regretted giving the young man a new set of nightmares to follow him in his dreams. On the other hand, with luck, West would live, and that was something—or as Justman had learned in his life and in his career…

It was everything.

It was a gift given to him by a starship captain named Rodriguez and the finest bridge crew he had ever known. It was given to him by countless others who fought and died for their beliefs—who fought and died for others.

It was a gift that Justman never felt worthy to receive because his sacrifices had never been as great. Yet, he had always remembered theirs and tried to make a difference.

A new sound was added to the room, the sound of movement. Justman raised his hands and waited.

He did not have to wait long. The Klingons appeared quickly, stepping out with disruptors pointed at him. They were wary of some trick.

Their leader spoke.

"You surrender to us? Earther?" he spat. "You must not know much about Klingons. Turn around. You will soon wish you had died in battle, Earther, when we are through with you."

Admiral Justman complied. As he did he felt time slow to a crawl. The seconds stretched out and the sounds around him died away, replaced by a peaceful silence.

If West continued pounding or the Klingons said anything else, Justman was not aware of it. He turned his head to look up. He saw through the transparent dome and saw the *Enterprise* sitting just outside of the drydock.

It was still the most beautiful sight he had ever seen. It was still a ship of dreams.

Then the past and present merged into one, the *Constitution* and the *Enterprise* merged into one...

One ship...

One dream.

And she had come to save them all.

Admiral Justman fired his phaser.

For a moment, there was nothing, no sound, no movement. Then there was as a large section of the dome above them flew into space.

Then there was rush of air as he felt the stars pull him off the floor...pull him closer.

Scotty could feel the *Enterprise* coming to life beneath his feet. Power flooded into the warp core faster than even its designers ever intended.

He stepped out of the turbolift and onto the bridge.

"Good to see you, Mr. Scott," Uhura said, smiling at him as he strode out of the turbolift and onto the *Enterprise* bridge. He noted that every face on the bridge was smiling as well, and looking to him.

"You too, Commander," he said.

Uhura moved quickly out of the command chair and took her place at the communications console.

He hit the com button on the command chair and said, "Scott to engineering. How are we doin' Mr. Kyle?"

"Warp core will be at full power in about thirty seconds," Kyle's voice said. The lieutenant sounded calm, but Scotty knew that the lad had had a bad time at the station. He had done his job, but Scott knew that the young man had paid his own price for what he had seen.

There was a pause and then Kyle said, "Warp engines to full power."

There was a collective sigh of relief.

"Full power to helm," Sulu announced.

"How long until shields and phaser banks are fully charged, Mr. Kyle?" Scott asked.

"Just a few minutes, sir," Kyle replied.

"Fine," Scotty said. "We will stand by. Scott out."

That done, he got up and walked over to the bridge engineering station. He ran a quick test of the warp system. Mr. Spock had been right again. A slight change in the intermix formula had insured that they avoided the temporal problems they had had the last time they had attempted the procedure, flinging them days into the past.

This time, the cold start of the warp core had not caused

any problems. And it had taken even less time. Now they would soon be ready to give the Klingons a little surprise.

"Helm," Scott said. "Stand ready on my command to engage the Klingon ship."

"Standing by," Scott said.

"Uhura, have we heard from the captain or Mr. Spock?" he asked.

"No, sir. No reports," she said.

Before she could ask, Scotty said, "Let them be. They will advise us when they are ready."

Scotty knew that their chances against the Klingon warship would improve if the station's defenses were at full power as well. Scotty knew that it would be easier to power up the newer *Enterprise* engines than the old starbase core. Plus, Mr. Spock already had done the calculations for the *Enterprise*. He would be working on the fly at the station with antiquated equipment.

"Sir," the acting science officer said. "We were just scanned by the Klingon vessel."

"Damn," Scott said, adding a few more Gaelic words under his breath. "They know we have warp power and that we will be at full power soon."

He didn't need to call down to Kyle to get the report. He knew the math. Shields and phasers were still charging. It would be a few minutes yet before they were at full power—or whatever would pass for full power on the still damaged *Enterprise*.

If they waited a few more seconds, the shields might actually survive a full-power disruptor blast or a torpedo hit.

Once.

But even if they survived a single hit, Scotty knew they would not likely survive a second, or a third. And the Klingons would throw everything they had at the *Enterprise.*

"Shall I raise shields?" Sulu asked.

"No," Scotty said. He knew it would do more harm than good to try to raise them when the system was still charging and was in its present condition.

"We'll wait," he said to the entire bridge crew's unanswered question.

But the Klingon ship knew they had power and knew they would very soon have weapons.

He waited, but he knew the *Enterprise* would be going into battle, very soon—whether she was ready or not.

Chapter Seventeen

THE DECK SHOOK under Kirk's feet. It felt like someone was firing on the station, or like a large explosion had detonated nearby.

A quick glance at the environmental control board told him that there had been a large and sudden decompression in the arboretum—where Admiral Justman and Lieutenant West had just been.

A sense of foreboding rose up, but Kirk forced it down. He had duties.

Then a red light began flashing on the sensor board on the next console.

"Ah...Captain Kirk," Marsilii said from his position near the access door. "We don't have much longer."

Kirk could hear more and more disruptor blasts coming from the breaches in the rapidly failing blast door. He ignored them.

He scanned the readouts. The screen measuring the Klingon vessel's power output was increasing—minutely, but it was increasing.

"Um, sir..." Marsilii's nervous voice said. "The Klingons, sir."

Scanners, Kirk realized—they were scanning the *Enterprise*. A quick look at another readout told him that the ship's warp engines were online. That meant weapons and other systems would be powering up.

And if the Klingons were scanning the ship they would know that.

Even as he saw the graph measuring the Klingons' tractor beam show a decrease, Kirk was in motion. He threw himself at the nearby panel that held the switch for Marsilii's jury-rigged plasma weapon.

If the Klingons broke away before he reached it, the weapon would have no effect—and the *Enterprise* would be nearly helpless.

His hand slammed down on the switch as a disruptor blast tore into a nearby panel. He heard and saw out of his peripheral vision that Marsilii was returning fire.

Without turning around, Kirk said, "Get inside!"

Then the captain raced for the access door and threw himself inside as disruptor fire nipped at his heels. Jumping to the side, he hit the control panel that would shut the door.

And nothing happened.

He hit it again. Still nothing.

"Disruptor fire," Marsilii said. "It must have damaged the door. We can make a run for it."

"No," Kirk said. "If they know we've gone, they will

coordinate with the others and have a squad waiting for us at the next exit. Go up the ladder, Ensign."

Kirk returned fire as the young man followed his order. He knew what the security officer was thinking. There was nothing up there except the airlock that led to the travel pod, and the pod was a death trap with the Klingon cruiser outside.

Yet, up Marsilii went.

Kirk returned the Klingon fire and then raced up the ladder after him.

At the top of the ladder, he said, "Watch the door, Ensign, and blast anything that comes through it."

Kirk looked over the travel-pod airlock control panel. Fortunately, it was clearly marked. As he heard Marsilii firing down toward the door, he hit the button that said Emergency Ejection. He watched through the window as explosive bolts tore away the seal between the station and the travel pod, blasting it, twisting and turning, into space.

"Hold your fire," Kirk called out.

"Captain Kirk?" Marsilii said, turning to watch the travel pod go.

"They won't look for us if they think we went that way," Kirk responded.

Of course, that left them with another problem. How could they get past the Klingons and out of this service area?

Kirk motioned Marsilii to be quiet and edged his way out onto the catwalk that ringed the top of the control room's inner shell.

Disruptor bolts occasionally tore up from the access door below, but they were exploratory in nature. The

Klingons saw that Kirk and Marsilii had stopped returning fire and were wary of a trick.

That would give Kirk and the ensign some time. Not much, but it might be enough.

Kirk led the way around the catwalk to the opposite side and saw the small airlock and access corridor below. The problem was that there was no ladder this time and the Klingons would soon start their way up the ladder by the airlock.

Climbing over the guardrail, Kirk stepped onto the control room's inner shell. The surface was bare metal, but it was crisscrossed with cables and relay boxes. If they were careful they could climb down without arousing the Klingons.

If they did it quietly and quickly—and didn't slip or fall...

Marsilii followed Kirk's silent command and the two men made their way slowly down the curved surface.

The climb went more smoothly than Kirk thought it would and they were down in less than a minute. But then Kirk could hear Klingon voices. He made a mental note to learn at least a few words of Klingon if he survived the next day.

As they approached the small airlock door, Kirk heard the sound of boots on the catwalk. He knew there was very little time, but he waited until he had the rhythm of the steps before he hit the control panel that opened the door.

The sound of the door was mostly masked by the Klingons' own sounds. Kirk hoped it was enough as he pushed Marsilii inside and followed. He took the same care closing the door.

"Can you lock them out, *quietly?*" he said.

Marsilii nodded and hit a sequence on the console. By then Kirk had opened the other door and was racing down the small corridor, his phaser out and ready.

He spared a glance behind him and saw Marsilii locking the outer door as well. Then they came to the next set of airlock doors and repeated the procedure.

Finally on the other side of the two airlocks, Kirk allowed himself to relax a bit. If the Klingons knew where they had gone, they didn't have a chance. There would be Klingons waiting for them at the exit. But Kirk did not think so; his instincts told him that they had gotten away clean.

Well, that was fine, he thought. Things had gone the Klingons' way up until now. A sudden stab of feeling came over him when he remembered the decompression in the arboretum.

The admiral had given them time, time to hide the crystals and time to use the plasma weapon against the Klingon ship. That time might well save the *Enterprise* as well.

He gave Marsilii a smile and said, "Nice work, Ensign."

"Thank you, sir," the security officer said. "I only hope the EM burst worked."

Kirk nodded. He badly wanted to know, himself, but he had another task to attend to. He flipped open his communicator and said, "Kirk to Spock."

"Spock here," came the immediate reply. The Vulcan's voice was calm, as if he were making a routine status report.

"Does the station have power?" Kirk asked.

"I am finishing computations now."

"Could you hurry up, Mr. Spock?" Kirk asked.

"I am hurrying, sir," Spock said dryly.

"How long?" Kirk asked.

"Three minutes to finish the computations and then just two more minutes for the warp core to warm up. Fortunately, the core's design—"

"Thank you, Mr. Spock. I look forward to hearing your report in person. Good luck. Kirk out," the captain said as he closed his communicator.

Spock would succeed. If the Klingon ship had been damaged and had not yet engaged the *Enterprise,* they might turn this battle around.

The captain flipped his communicator open again and said, "Kirk to *Enterprise.*"

With Fuller in the lead, Kell, Parrish, and Clancy raced down the corridor and up the stairs they had been racing down just a few minutes ago.

Once inside the first stairwell, Fuller blasted the control panel for the door. It would not hold the Klingons for long, but it would help. It might buy Spock and Jawer a few extra seconds to work their miracle.

Battles were won and lost by seconds, Kell knew. He had seen it. And he had seen those precious seconds bought with the blood of brave people, brave warriors. He was willing to shed his own blood for whatever advantage it would bring. He knew the other three with him were just as willing.

They did the same thing on five more levels, then another. Kell's blood warned him that the Klingon force must be close.

At the stop of another stairwell, Fuller stopped and turned around. Clearly he was thinking the same thing.

"We need to stop their descent on this deck," he said. "Stand back."

The group moved back while Fuller stood in front of the doors they had just exited and fired his phaser inside. He fired a long blast and then stepped away from the doors and fired again. The red beam crumpled the metal, twisting it and throwing it into the ruined stairwell.

"That will keep them from even trying that way down. Come on," he said, gesturing down the corridor. They followed, and Fuller did the same thing to the next stairwell.

Then the next.

Finally, at the end of the corridor, there were large doors that were at least ten meters high and twice that wide. The sign on top of the door said, MANUFACTURING PLANT.

"This is where we make our stand. Come on," Fuller said, stepping inside. Kell, Parrish, and Clancy followed.

The manufacturing facility was large, very large. It was roughly a square of about two hundred meters in length and width. At the far end were a large stairwell and a freight turbolift that probably took heavy equipment to the lower levels of the station.

The space between was nearly covered with synthesizers, metallurgy equipment, consoles, and other equipment whose function Kell could only guess at.

It was large, and it had many obstructions. In many ways it would provide great advantages to the defenders.

However, Kell knew they would be fighting a larger force of highly trained and very aggressive Klingon warriors. These were no simpleminded and arrogant Orions.

"We have to stop them from getting to that stairwell," Fuller said, pointing to the rear of the room. "We need to hold them as long as we can then fall back in that direction. In the event that we are overrun and you are the only one of use left, overload your phaser and toss it inside. If they can't get down that way, they will have to backtrack two sectors to find another way down. Remember, to win, we don't have to beat them, we just have to buy Mr. Spock and Ensign Jawer enough time to get the warp core and the station's defenses back online.

"Come on," Fuller said, "we have to find our positions quickly."

The first stop that the chief made was the rear of the room, where he tested the freight turbolift. The doors opened and there was a car there, but it would not move.

"Good, so there's only one way down to engineering," he said. "Anderson, you're with me. Parrish and Clancy, take position on the right," he said, pointing to a large piece of equipment. "Get up high, if you can. It will be another advantage."

Then Fuller led Kell to the left side of the room near the front, where they chose a large console. Fuller boosted Kell up, and then Kell gave the chief a hand. Moments later, they were in position, looking down from the console's three-meter height.

Kell scanned with his eyes and found Parrish and Clancy, atop another piece of equipment. For a moment, he caught Parrish's eyes. Neither moved, or made an expression, yet something passed between them. Against all sense and reason, Kell found himself thinking of the future.

Then the moment passed and both looked forward. Their future would be mere minutes unless they could get out of this room alive. He knew it was intended for building things, creation. Yet in a few moments, he knew it would be full of destruction and death.

It would become a killing box.

Kell waited and watched the door.

"Scott here, Captain," Scotty replied. "It is good to hear your voice, sir."

"Yours too, Mr. Scott. The ship?" Kirk asked.

"Fine, sir. The Klingons scanned us and we thought... well, we thought it was over. Then the Klingons got a nasty shock. I assume that was you. I thought I recognized your work, Captain."

"Not me, Mr. Scott. You will have to thank a young ensign from the station for that pulse."

"Then I look forward to shaking his hand."

"I will try to arrange that, Mr. Scott. What is the ship's status?"

"We'll have phasers and shields fully charged soon," Scott said.

"All systems at full power," the acting science officer announced.

"We are ready, Captain," Scott said. "We can engage the Klingon ship right now if you give the word."

"Delay that," Kirk said. "Do not fire unless the Klingons fire at the *Enterprise*. They were powering down their tractor beam when we hit them. I'm not sure they have been incapacitated. If you can, wait for Mr. Spock to get the station to full power."

"Aye, sir," Scotty said.

"Good work, Mr. Scott," Kirk said.

"Thank you, sir," Scotty said, then the captain broke the connection.

"Monitor the Klingons very carefully," Scotty said to the acting science officer. "I want to know if the commander uses the head."

"Aye, sir," came the reply.

Up until now, the day had been defined by defeat after defeat. Setback after setback.

But something had happened when the captain's team had struck at the Klingons. They weren't invincible, as it had started to seem.

If the Klingons could suffer one setback, they could suffer another, and another.

The tide of the battle had turned. Scotty was sure of it. Just as he was sure that no one could dish out setbacks like Captain Kirk.

Chapter Eighteen

"ARE YOU READY, Mr. Spock?" Ensign Jawer asked.

Spock could hear the nervous tension in the young human's voice. That tension had increased when the disruptor fire had begun on the engineering section's door. The Vulcan had found the disruptor fire a distraction.

He would have preferred complete silence for his calculations. The new intermix formula he had developed had been optimized for the *Enterprise*'s mass and its warp engine's output.

Both of those variables were different on the station. In addition, scans of the warp core itself told Spock that it was no longer operating according to specifications. And to make matters more difficult, his scans showed that it would be subject to fluctuations in its own power output.

Those new variables required careful computations.

While the Vulcan would have preferred quiet, ignoring the noise of the disruptors was a simple matter of mental discipline—a discipline that Jawer, as most humans, seemed to lack.

"Mr. Spock?" Jawer said again.

The Vulcan turned away from his work for a moment to face the human. "If it reduces your anxiety, I have calculated that the Klingons will not be able to penetrate the door for at least twelve minutes at their current rate of fire," he said.

"What?" Jawer said, his face showing that the information did not reduce his anxiety at all.

"Ensign," Spock said. "Anxiety is counterproductive and at the moment, illogical. We still have nearly twelve minutes before the Klingons break through the door."

Spock returned to his work. There was just a final check on his calculations.

"Complete," Spock said.

The human smiled. "What can I do?" Jawer asked.

"I will begin the intermix countdown from here," Spock said. "Please observe the dilithium reaction chamber for irregularities."

The human sprinted for the dilithium chamber, which was several meters away from Spock's engineering panel.

"Ten seconds," Spock said.

"All systems seem normal," Jawer announced.

Spock nodded.

"Five," he said.

"Four.

"Three.

"Two.

"One."

Spock could hear the hum of the dilithium reaction chamber as it powered up. Then a warning alarm went off.

"Mr. Spock, something's wrong," Jawer said.

"I know, Ensign," the Vulcan said.

The readouts in front of him detailed the problem.

"What can I do?" the human asked.

"Nothing at the moment," Spock said as he adjusted the control. He tried to slow down the reaction, since stopping it was impossible.

"What's wrong?" Jawer said from beside him.

"The dilithium chamber is too cold," Spock said.

"I thought this was a cold-start procedure?" the human asked.

"It is," Spock said, "Relatively speaking. Unfortunately, it requires a minimum temperature that the system's plasma injectors do not seem able to provide in the time we have."

"How *unfortunately,* sir?" Jawer asked.

"The reactor will go critical if the reaction continues for another two minutes and forty-one seconds," Spock said.

"So what can we do?" Jawer said.

"At the moment nothing," Spock said. "The plasma injectors are not operating according to specifications. The reaction will result in a cascade failure that will lead to the release of extreme radiation and the inevitable violent explosion of the warp core. Of course, fail-safe systems will no doubt eject the warp core before that happens."

"That is a worst-case scenario, right sir?" Jawer asked.

"Unfortunately, no. That is what will happen in the next two minutes and seven seconds."

"Unless...?" the human said expectantly.

"I am afraid that there is little we can do to stop it. An upgrade or repair of the plasma injectors would take substantially more time than we have," Spock said.

"So that's it?" Jawer said. "No power to the weapons? A huge explosion right here?"

"I am afraid so, Ensign," Spock said. "It is unfortunate."

Then Jawer was on the move, racing for the dilithium chamber. "I have an idea," he said, taking out his phaser.

"That is unlikely to work, Mr. Jawer," Spock said.

"But it would be illogical not to try—under the circumstances," Jawer said, as he pulled open the outer panel of one of the plasma injectors.

"True," Spock said. He checked his readouts and then said, "Use no higher than a heavy stun setting."

"Yes, sir," Jawer said as he adjusted his phaser.

Though the odds were against it, Spock did see that there was a possibility it would work. He shunted power to the power-transfer conduits and tried to slow the reaction.

"On my mark," Spock said.

"Yes, sir," the human replied.

The Vulcan watched the readouts carefully. It was impossible to compute all of the variables, so he simply said, "Fire phaser."

He heard the whine of a hand phaser and saw the immediate effect on the temperature of the plasma stream.

It was rising. Spock shunted more power to the transfer conduits.

The temperature rose again.

His ears told him that the ensign was maintaining consistent fire. Spock could see that the reaction was slowing slightly and the temperature was rising steadily inside the chamber.

Spock disabled the fail-safe systems. If he did not, then the warp core would eject automatically.

Then the reaction became self-sustaining. In a moment he would see if it remained within operational parameters or if it would become a runaway reaction.

If that happened, the warp core would go critical while it was still inside the station. All the antimatter in the large reactor would immediately be freed from its magnetic containment and would then react with the surrounding matter of the station.

The starbase would see a matter-antimatter reaction that was many orders of magnitude higher than that in a photon torpedo. The Vulcan regretted that he would not see it. To his knowledge, such a large explosive reaction had never occurred. It would no doubt be a fascinating sight.

The reaction spiked for a moment, and then came under control. The immediate danger was past. Then he saw the feedback wave beginning in the plasma injectors. Though the injectors were no longer necessary to sustain the reaction, there was another danger.

"Ensign!" Spock called out. The Vulcan turned his head to see the blast take Ensign Jawer full in the chest and throw him several meters backward.

Spock could not leave his control panel at the moment. He still had to manage the reaction manually to insure that there was no further danger. In any case, a quick calculation told him there was a very small chance that the human had survived.

Ensign Jawer had taken a very logical risk. He had traded his own life for the lives of the people on the station, and the larger number of people in the Federation that might suffer if they failed.

It was logical, yet unfortunate, the Vulcan thought.

A few moments later, Spock saw the reaction level out. He reinstated the fail-safe systems, and then turned his attention to the door, which was beginning to show signs of buckling under the strain of constant disruptor fire.

A single switch on his control panel turned on the forcefield that protected the outer door. Immediately, the sound of disruptor fire was dulled. The Klingons would now need days to break through the shield with hand disruptors.

Spock immediately routed power to the station's shields and weapons systems. The station defenses would be back online shortly.

Then he turned his attention to Ensign Jawer. As Spock approached him more closely, he saw that the human had indeed taken the force of the blast to the chest.

Spock could see burns radiating from the central wound in his sternum. Remarkably, the Vulcan could also see that the human was breathing.

Kneeling down, he saw that Jawer was unconscious. To Spock's surprise, his pulse was strong.

Remarkable, the Vulcan thought.

He made the human as comfortable as he could and then returned to his console to call the *Enterprise.*

Kirk did not hesitate. He stepped in front of the door to the corridor with his phaser ready. When the door opened automatically, he stepped through it. There were no Klingons to be seen in the corridor.

They had gotten away clean.

The captain refused to congratulate himself, however. He had seen the tide working against them too many times in the last few hours to think that their recent successes guaranteed anything. And he would not underestimate the Klingons.

There were still a dozen things that could go wrong. He would not allow overconfidence to add to their possible handicaps.

He motioned Marsilii to follow him, and the two men moved quickly through the corridor. The ensign had indicated that there was an emergency turbolift that went directly to the auxiliary control deck just a few hundred meters down the corridor and around the corner.

Kirk held out little hope that the turbolift would be functioning. However, it would have an emergency stairwell nearby. The stairs would take precious time, but they would get there.

At the intersection of the corridors, Kirk stopped and carefully peeked his head around the corner.

There was a squad of at least seven Klingons waiting there. For what Kirk did not know. They had the look of officers waiting for orders.

He slowly pulled his head back. The fact that he was in motion already was the only thing that saved him.

One of the Klingons saw him, raised his disruptor with incredible speed, and fired in one very quick and very smooth motion. Kirk got his head out of the line of fire a fraction of a second before it sent metal from the corridor flying.

He heard the unmistakable sound of Klingon boots running on the corridor floor.

"Pull back and find cover," Kirk said, turning to run.

Less then twenty meters away, they found station support pylons for cover. Splitting up, they took positions on either side of the corridor, with Marsilii on Kirk's right side.

Spinning around, Kirk started firing down the corridor before he could even see where he was aiming. Not surprisingly, when he was able to get a look, he saw that he had not hit anything.

Marsilii, apparently, did not have any luck either.

From what Kirk could see, the Klingons had found cover behind pylons as well—about sixty yards down the corridor. They began firing immediately.

Kirk couldn't wait for a lull in the enemy fire, because there was none. Every few seconds, he had to lean away from his cover and fire on the Klingons and quickly duck back.

A quick glance told him that Marsilii was doing the same with the same result.

Kirk knew that this kind of fighting could continue indefinitely. The chance of hitting someone in a covered position was slim. It would take many shots and some luck to catch someone when they leaned out to fire.

Of course, the Klingons outnumbered them eight to one, so they would win a fight if it became a battle of attrition. On the other hand, if they had called for reinforcements, the fight would end even more quickly if Klingons rushed Kirk and Marsilii from behind.

In either case, Kirk could not afford to wait. He and Marsilii were the only ones who knew that Spock was getting the station's power online and they were likely the only ones in a position to get to the auxiliary control room.

Kirk knew what he had to do.

He quickly adjusted his phaser to overload. According to the *Starfleet Survival Manual* he was supposed to throw the weapon clear immediately. However, he did not want to risk giving the Klingons time to run for cover. He needed to get them all in one blast or they might never get to the auxiliary control room.

So Kirk listened to the pitch of the overload and waited until the last possible second. Leaning into the corridor, he pitched the phaser forward. He immediately pulled back and heard the explosion as he did so.

There was a brief pressure as the concussion wave passed his position as it traveled down the corridor.

Kirk glanced across the corridor to see that Marsilii was unhurt. The ensign nodded and Kirk leaned to the side to see if any of the Klingons were still there.

A quick count told him that there were eight motionless bodies on the floor, and Kirk motioned Marsilii to move out.

Kirk headed down the corridor at a run. He stopped only for a moment to pick up a fallen Klingon disruptor.

Then he and Marsilii were dashing down the corridor and made a quick turn, barreling for the turbolift and emergency stairs.

Kirk stopped in front of the lift, and to his surprise it opened.

Marsilii was right behind him and Kirk turned to see the ensign enter the lift. He said, "Auxiliary control," but before he had finished the command a disruptor bolt flashed from somewhere and tore into Marsilii from the back while he was in the middle of turning around.

Reflexively, Kirk leaned forward and caught the young man, who had been propelled into the turbolift wall and was slowly sliding down.

In an instant Kirk could see that the wound in the dead center of the young man's back was fatal.

Yet Marsilii sputtered for a moment and Kirk lowered him slowly to the floor.

Kirk could see that the ensign was fading fast. Looking him in the eye, Kirk said, "You did very well, Ensign. The station is going to make it."

For a moment, Marsilii looked completely lucid and said, "Thank you, sir," and died.

Closing the security officer's eyes, the captain leaned him carefully against the wall.

A moment later, the turbolift came to a stop and Kirk was on his feet and out the door. He could see the auxiliary control room doors. He did not bother with caution and raced for them.

There were no Klingons in sight and the doors opened automatically. Auxiliary control was empty. Kirk guessed that officers who had been there had tried to defend the station against the Klingons.

He headed immediately to the weapons console. Both shields and weapons showed full power. He allowed himself a small smile and remembered the price that others had paid for this success. Ensign Marsilii and both Admiral Justman and Lieutenant West—and many more, he had no doubt.

Kirk hit the button to turn the shields on and opened his communicator.

"Kirk to *Enterprise*," he said as he called up a view of the Klingon ship on the screen in front of him.

Chapter Nineteen

WHEN THE KLINGONS CAME, they did not just come through the door, they came through the wall. They must have brought or improvised some sort of explosives, Kell realized.

The door exploded inward, as did another four or five meters of wall on either side of it.

That complicated things. Now, instead of picking off the attackers as they came through the door, Kell and the others were faced with a row of perhaps a dozen Klingon warriors, who charged through the smoke.

Kell's phaser was firing before he was consciously aware of it. Fuller's was as well. Both men found targets quickly. He also saw phaser blasts come from Parrish and Clancy's direction.

For a moment, the Klingons were caught unaware by the fire from above. Kell and the others kept their fire in short bursts as they had been trained to do. This made it harder for the Klingons to trace the origin points of the blasts.

The advantage allowed the Starfleet officers to strike target after target. Perhaps a dozen of the Klingons fell in short order, but more warriors rushed to replace them.

More fell and the smoke near the entrance grew thicker.

Suddenly a Klingon voice called for the warriors to cease fire. Kell stayed his own hand. Fuller and the others—who did not understand the command—kept up their blasts, giving away their position.

More Klingons fell, but a shouting Klingon voice, which Kell realized must belong to their commander, gave the Klingon warriors fairly accurate coordinates.

Only a few warriors made it through to covered positions, but those warriors aimed a barrage of disruptor fire at the console that Kell and Fuller fired down from. The two men had to cease fire and pull back for a moment.

Turning his head, Kell saw that Parrish and Clancy were facing a similar barrage from another group of Klingons firing from a second position.

"They have us," Fuller called out loud enough for Parrish and Clancy to hear. "Pull back."

Then there was another order shouted in Klingon and the disruptor bolts changed their angle and started striking the ceiling and support beams above the two Starfleet positions.

Sparks and debris began to rain down on Fuller and Kell as they crawled backward. Whoever their commander was, Kell realized, he was no Orion fool.

At the back of the console, Fuller and Kell wasted no

time. They leapt to the floor. "There," Fuller said, pointing to a tall and wide synthesizer unit. It was about three meters across, and the two men took positions on either side.

Kell fired and he could hear Fuller's beams as well as other phaser fire that he knew belonged to Parrish and Clancy. Once again, he was reminded of Kahless and his Lady Lukura fighting side by side, withstanding the attack of five hundred warriors.

He thought Parrish might understand that story, and he found that he hoped they would both live long enough that he could tell it to her.

Disruptor fire tore into the synthesizer that shielded them, but Kell immediately saw why the chief had chosen it as cover. The synthesizer seemed nearly indestructible, which made sense since it needed to withstand the incredible heat and energies inside.

Kell's ears told him that one of the phasers from Parrish's position had gone silent. Turning his head to see if Parrish had been hit, he saw her maintaining her fire. At first, he thought that Clancy must have been hit; then he saw the ensign working feverishly at a console.

She called to Parrish, who stopped firing and turned to Clancy, who gave Fuller and Kell a hand signal telling them that she had rigged the equipment somehow.

"Chief!" Kell called out.

"I saw it," Fuller replied. "We'll wait for their signal."

Kell maintained his fire, noting that the Klingons were advancing on Parrish and Clancy's former position. By now, the two females had disappeared from his view.

Finally, they heard Clancy shout, "Get down!"

Kell automatically dropped to the floor and covered his head with his hands, as he heard Fuller doing the same.

There was a large explosion that made the deck under him shudder and sent a blast of heat over his head. Kell held his breath for as long as he could to make sure that he did not take in the superheated air.

Finally judging it safe, Kell took a breath and saw that the exploding heavy equipment had cleared the immediate area of Klingons...and pretty much everything else for a twenty-meter radius.

He suspected that any Klingons within an even greater circle were now dead or injured.

Kell's suspicions were confirmed when he noted that there was no more disruptor fire coming from that side of the manufacturing plant.

The Klingons who remained concentrated their fire on Kell and the chief's position. The two men returned fire, but Kell could see the Klingons were beginning to advance.

"Pull back," Fuller said.

Turning, Kell followed the chief, who ran toward a new position behind a less than two-meter-high console, the function of which Kell could only guess.

They were getting closer to the back wall of the large plant. Scanning quickly, he saw that Parrish and Clancy were even closer to the wall. Neither team would have long before they had no remaining fallback positions.

Kell found that the prospect did not trouble him. He had seen Fuller, other security officers, and even himself succeed in more difficult circumstances.

Klingons were taught that the only victory was victory. But he had seen humans win impossible victories simply by not conceding defeat, by buying time—sometimes minutes, sometimes seconds—time to think of something, time for help to arrive. They preserved life for the last possible microsecond and maintained their belief that while there was life there was hope.

Kell had found that human beliefs were strong, and apparently contagious.

"Hold your fire," Fuller said. "Let's not announce ourselves until they are closer."

For a moment, the room was quiet.

Kell spared a glance at Parrish and Clancy, who were behind another large piece of equipment. Clancy was busy working at the console, and Kell knew that she was preparing another surprise for the attackers.

An instant before it happened, Kell's blood screamed a warning. On his blood's call alone, he looked about twenty meters behind the females and saw two Klingons making their way quietly into a firing position.

Cursing the crafty Klingon in command, he swung his phaser around and called out, "Down! Behind you!"

Parrish was fast, but she did not use her speed to duck. Instead, she spun around and was firing before the echo of Kell's words had died.

Clancy was almost as fast, but not fast enough to avoid the disruptor blast that tore into her left shoulder.

The blast turned her shoulder into a ruined mess and threw her body back into the console she had been working a moment before.

Kell fired and hit one of the Klingons, while Parrish

eliminated the other. Kell allowed himself a deep breath and thought the danger was past.

Then he saw Clancy stagger forward, trying to focus as she held out her phaser. Then the ensign was falling, firing her phaser as she did.

Again, Parrish reacted quickly, but instead of avoiding the danger, she reached out for her partner.

The beam cut into the underside of Parrish's right arm, then Clancy fell to the floor and her phaser slid away.

Kell was stepping toward Parrish before Clancy hit the floor. Leslie was dazed and trying to work her right hand, which still held the phaser but wouldn't respond.

Parrish sank to her knees and started to lean. She would have fallen but Kell was there in an instant.

He reached behind her, being careful not to put any pressure on the injured right arm. Quickly inspecting the damage, he saw that she had sustained a serious phaser burn on her arm. The skin was damaged and probably some muscle underneath. It was nothing Dr. McCoy could not repair.

She would live, if he found a way to make sure she survived the battle. He had to do something quickly. Scanning the area around him, he knew what he had to do.

"Jon," Parrish said.

"You're going to be all right," he said. "I'm going to get you to safety."

He reached behind her and prepared to pick her up, when she stopped him with her good hand.

"Clancy," she said.

He looked over his shoulder. Clancy was not moving.

"I think she's—" he began.

"Make sure," she said, iron in her voice. Carefully, he leaned her kneeling figure against the console and ran to Clancy's position. Crouching above her, he saw that her wound was terrible and her eyes were staring up at the ceiling. Still, he felt quickly for a pulse and found none. Ensign Clancy was beyond help.

He turned back to Parrish when he remembered something. Twisting his body back, he grabbed for Clancy's phaser.

"Chief," he called out and slid the phaser to Fuller, who acknowledged him with a nod and reached for the weapon even as he kept up his own fire.

Kell rushed back to Parrish, who had transferred her phaser to her good hand and was trying to raise it.

"No," he said firmly. "You have done your part."

Then he lifted her off the floor and carried her at a run to the door to the freight turbolift. When he stepped in front, the lift doors opened obediently. Placing her gently on the floor in a sitting position, he made sure that she had a firm grip on the phaser.

"Jon," she said, her voice a whisper.

"Leslie," he said. "You will be fine. Wait here and use the phaser if you have to."

He turned to go.

"Wait," she said, and he stopped, turning back to her. He leaned down and kissed her fiercely, passionately and tenderly. She returned it all.

When he pulled back she looked intensely at him and said, "Come back."

He looked at her, his Lady Lukara, and smiled.

"Promise me you will come back," she said.

Kell returned her gaze and said, "I promise." It was the last lie he would allow himself in this world, he vowed.

Yet it seemed to bring her comfort and he judged it worthwhile. He took one last look at her, then raced out of the turbolift and back into the battle.

Back into the killing box.

Chapter Twenty

KIRK SAW THE KLINGON SHIP moving on the viewscreen on the weapons panel in front of him. He immediately put down the communicator and quickly familiarized himself with the control panel.

As he switched on the targeting scanners, he saw the Klingon vessel swing around in a rapid arc, firing its disruptors at the *Enterprise.*

The battle had begun.

Even as the *Enterprise* executed an aggressive evasive maneuver, his ship fired one and then another torpedo. Kirk noted with pride that both torpedoes made nearly direct hits on the Klingon ship's shields, while the disruptor fire missed the starship entirely.

The targeting scanners took some adjusting to give him a lock, taking up precious seconds. Looking up again, he saw the Klingon vessel turn sharply and out of the viewer's range.

Kirk found the tracking control and hit it. The view switched to somewhere Kirk guessed was under the station. Then the Klingon cruiser shot up in a very tight arc.

Hitting the firing control, Kirk fired the station's phasers at the Klingon warship. The phaser beam missed its target. In fact, Kirk could see that the beam had not even come close.

Muttering some nonregulation language, Kirk turned off the computer targeting and put the weapons system on manual.

Then he watched as the station's external cameras tracked the Klingon ship. It banked sharply and fired a combination of torpedoes at the station. The deck shook under Kirk's feet and for a moment the station's external cameras lost sight of the Klingon vessel.

When the Klingon ship appeared again on the viewscreen, it seemed to be barreling straight for the viewscreen. Green disruptor fire flared from the warship and the shield-failure alarm began to sound on the board.

Then the Klingon cruiser veered away from the starbase and fired a spread of torpedoes at the *Enterprise*.

Two Klingon torpedoes hit the *Enterprise*'s shields, and Kirk winced as he saw the ship's shields flare a brilliant violet. They were weakening, he knew.

Quickly studying the board in front of him, Kirk noted that there were nine phaser emitters spaced at equidistant points on the outer ring of the station. Using manual control, he could target each of them individually.

Since the starbase's phasers were relatively low-powered, that was important. He would have to achieve a sustained hit to be effective against the Klingon shields.

He saw the Klingon vessel's disruptors strike the *Enterprise;* then the Klingon warship got into a new position behind the station.

Kirk could immediately see the Klingon commander's plan. He was keeping close to the starbase, counting on the *Enterprise* to be reluctant to fire weapons when there was a chance of hitting the station.

Of course, there were Klingons on the station as well, but that fact did not seem to trouble the Klingon commander.

Tracking the Klingon ship carefully, Kirk anticipated the commander's next maneuver.

Perfect, he thought as the Klingon ship began a sharp arc around the station, following what was almost an orbit along the starbase's plane.

He reached for the controls for two of the station's phaser emitters. Firing both, he was pleased to see them both strike the Klingon ship's shields.

Already committed to the maneuver, the Klingon ship continued on its trajectory. Kirk tracked it, firing phaser banks in sequence around the station. He was always able to keep at least one phaser beam on the Klingon ship and often was able to keep two at once.

Finally, the Klingon ship changed direction, twisting violently up and away from the plane of the station. Kirk tracked it, keeping two phasers locked on and firing continuously.

Then the *Enterprise* was there, firing a full burst of

photon torpedoes. One…two…three torpedoes struck the Klingon ship's struggling shields, which collapsed in a flash of red light.

Scotty did not waste any time. A series of precise phaser beams lanced out at the Klingon forward torpedo tube, then at the right and left nacelles, which Kirk knew housed the disruptor banks as well as the ship's warp drive.

Swinging around, the starship struck the Klingon ship's rear torpedo tubes with phasers, and Kirk knew the ship was no longer a threat.

"Kirk to *Enterprise*," the captain said.

"Scott here," Scotty's voice replied.

"Excellent work, Scotty. Precision shooting," Kirk said.

"That was some precision shooting down there. Your work, Captain?" the chief engineer replied.

"All the real work was done by the other officers, Mr. Scott," Kirk said. "The ones that didn't make it."

"Aye," Scott said.

"Status of the Klingon ship?" Kirk asked.

"Sensors show that they have lost warp power and all weapons systems. They won't be troubling us anymore," Scotty replied. "And our sensors show that most of the fighting on the station has stopped."

Kirk wondered if that was because the Klingons were standing down or if there was just no one left to resist them.

"Captain," Scotty said. "This is a surprise. The Klingon commander is requesting permission to begin beaming his people back to the ship."

Kirk thought about that for a moment. It seemed unusual, but anything to get the Klingons off the station. There was still the problem of what to do with a ship full of Klingons, but at least they would all be in one place.

"Let them begin transport, but watch them carefully, Scotty," Kirk said. "I've had enough surprises from Klingons for one day."

"I'm getting a report..." Scotty said. "Sir, there is a Klingon cruiser coming in at high warp."

It was not over, Kirk realized.

"How long?" Kirk said.

"Less than one hour," Scotty replied.

"Get as much power to shields and phasers as you can, Mr. Scott. And begin search and rescue operations on the station. I will also need a repair crew over here to try to get power to the starbase's shields."

An hour wasn't much time, Kirk knew. He hoped the teams would find some survivors before the other Klingon ship arrived. On the other hand, he was not sure the *Enterprise* could protect them.

Still, they had an hour to make repairs. Perhaps Scotty could restore the station's shields. The station and ship had defeated one Klingon cruiser. They could defeat another.

"Sir, there's a communication for you from Starfleet Command," Scotty said.

"Have Uhura patch it to auxiliary control at the station," Kirk said.

"Aye, Scott out," the chief engineer said.

A moment later Admiral Solow's face appeared on the viewscreen. "Captain Kirk, what is your status?"

* * *

A phaser beam tore into the equipment in front of Karel. Then another tore into the warrior beside him.

"Arghhhh!" Karel shouted in his rage.

The warriors he fought with had fought well, but the honorless and cowardly Earthers had struck down too many good warriors.

Now there were more reasons to take vengeance.

Karel could smell his victory, though he cursed the Earthers for making the cost of it so high and the time required to take it so long.

The small band had kept him from accessing the stairs down to the engineering level. That would soon stop; there were two, perhaps three of them left.

And soon he would see the last of them die. Then he would deal with the troublesome Earthers who had locked themselves in with the warp core.

He called out to Gash, and the large Klingon turned, his one remaining eye burning with rage, mirroring the burning in Karel's own blood.

Soon the Earthers would feel that fire.

"Take those warriors," he said, pointing to the Klingons firing nearly continuously on the Earthers' position.

Then there was a buzzing sound. In his battle fury, it took him a moment to place the familiar sound.

Then he reached for his communicator and pulled it out.

"What do you want?" he barked.

"Return to the ship, disengage the Earthers," the com officer's voice spat back.

For a moment, Karel could not believe what he had just heard.

"Repeat!" he shouted.

"Move your warriors away from that protected area. You need to find a place near the exterior hull for beam-out. Captain Koloth's order. Comply immediately!"

"What is it?" Gash asked him.

"We are ordered to return to the ship," Karel said.

"The battle is not finished," Gash shouted.

"No, it is not," Karel said, "but it soon will be."

He ordered the Klingons in the room to pull back and collect around him. There were eight warriors left. Their losses were great indeed.

"Gash, take the remaining warriors to a position near the external hull for beam-out," Karel said.

"What about you?" Gash said.

"I will stay and finish the Earthers," Karel said.

Gash did not look pleased and his single eye still burned. Yet, he turned and led the other seven warriors back out the way they had come.

Karel took a few seconds to scan the wreckage of the complex in front of him. His eyes and ears did not reveal where the Earthers were now.

But his blood did.

Then his ears told him someone was approaching him from behind.

He barely stayed his hand and stopped himself from reducing Gash to atoms.

"I ordered you to go with the others!" Karel shouted.

Gash smiled. "And the captain ordered you to return to the ship," he said.

"We will have to face our reprimands later," Karel said. "I know where the Earthers are."

Kirk finished making his report of the day's event to the silver-haired Starfleet admiral. The captain had never met the man before, but he knew his record, or, rather, his legend.

"And, Admiral, I do not think that Admiral Justman made it," Kirk said.

Something touched the admiral's face, the first expression Kirk had seen since the transmission had begun.

Then Admiral Solow's reserve reasserted itself and he said, "We lost a lot of good people today, Captain Kirk."

"Too many, sir," Kirk said.

"But you did some fine work down there. You and your people have done more for the Federation than you realize," Solow said.

"Thank you, sir, but the ones who did the most are no longer here," Kirk said.

"That's always the way it is, Captain," Solow said. "All we can do is honor their memory and the things they fought for."

"Standing by for your orders," Kirk said.

"You should know that I have just received a call from the Klingon command. They are disavowing any knowledge of the actions of the Klingon battle cruiser *D'k tahg*."

"What?" Kirk asked. "That cannot be. The attack on the station was part of a coordinated effort by Klingon command. It began with the incidents in System 1324 and the mine in 7348."

"You and I are in complete agreement there, but officially we have to accept the Klingon story," Solow said. Then, before Kirk could protest, the admiral said, "You are to release the *D'k tahg* to the Klingon ship currently on its way to your position."

"Sir, a lot of people gave their lives to stop the Klingons here today," Kirk said.

"And they did stop them, you all did. But the most important thing you have bought for us is time. Time to prepare, time to try to make sure that what you have all been through and sacrificed for today is not replayed throughout the Federation."

Kirk nodded. He knew the admiral was right, but he hated the notion of simply letting the Klingons go.

"We have no choice," Kirk said.

"No, if the war begins today we cannot be sure that we will win. However, neither are the Klingons or this would have been a much bigger operation than a raid on a single, nearly obsolete starbase."

"I understand, sir," Kirk said.

"Please also understand that we will not forget what happened here today, Captain, and there will be another time and another place. We will finish what began in System 1324. And when we do fight, we will fight to win."

"The *Enterprise* will be ready, sir," Kirk said.

Chapter Twenty-one

BEFORE KELL FOUND SAM FULLER with his eyes, his ears told him how the fight was going.

And how it would end.

The disruptor blasts were coming quickly now, and from many different places. Fuller was firing both phasers nearly continuously.

"Chief," he called as he rejoined the human.

"Good to see you, Jon," Fuller said as Kell took a position next to him.

"You too, sir," Kell replied, taking aim and firing in one smooth motion.

The Klingon warriors were moving quickly on them now, as a *targ* does when it senses its prey weakening. Then, suddenly, the disruptor fire stopped for several seconds.

"Let's pull back," Fuller said. They were at the last

piece of cover before the wall that was the end of the manufacturing plant. Less than twenty meters away was the door that would lead the Klingons to the engineering level.

Fuller pointed back behind them. They would move away from the door, but find more cover and still have a line of fire on any Klingons making for the stairwell.

It was the only move left to them. Kell knew it would likely be their last maneuver, the last order that Sam Fuller would give him.

The Klingon commander was planning something. Kell's blood boiled with the danger.

Still, there was nothing to do but follow Chief Sam Fuller to the new position and follow this fight to the end and straight to the River of Blood.

Both men were on their feet and made the ten meters to the next covered position quickly. Kell was surprised that there was no disruptor fire on their heels.

Kell and Fuller took their positions behind a large support pylon and waited, scanning the wrecked machine shop around them and straining their ears for any sign of their attackers.

They had a clean line of sight to the stairwell door, but there was no movement.

Then the silence was broken by a high-pitched whine. For a moment, Kell could not place the sound. Before the meaning of the sound registered in his mind, Sam Fuller was screaming, "Down!" Then Kell felt a weight on him.

The overloaded disruptor exploded loudly and with great force, but the real damage was done by the pile of raw polymers that was nearby.

They were turned into a hundred projectiles and Kell felt them pierce his skin in a dozen places.

He took a moment to inventory his body and decided that none of the wounds were fatal.

"Jon, are you okay?" Fuller said.

"Yes, sir," Jon said as he felt the chief's weight disappear. Then Kell was on his knees. He tested the grip on his phaser to make certain that his hand still worked despite the wound on his forearm.

His hand functioned. He could still fight.

"Careful, they're moving," Fuller said.

Then Kell looked up and saw that Fuller had taken the brunt of the explosion. His right side was riddled with small punctures, yet none of them explained the growing pool of blood on the floor at the chief's feet.

Then Kell saw the wound on the side of Fuller's neck. It was not large, but Kell knew enough of human anatomy to know that it was enough.

The chief saw something in Kell's eyes and raised his hand to the wound. Then Kell could see that the human understood.

Kell's mind raced. The chief had minutes, or less. But if they could break the Klingon line, get to the corridor, there might be medical supplies...

"Jon," Fuller said. "Something's different. Most of them are gone. They are coming from that direction." Fuller pointed to the area thirty meters ahead and just to the left of the door.

"Chief, we can rush them, then we'll get you—"

"No," Fuller said. "This part of the fight is mine."

"But—"

"That's an order," Fuller said, and swayed slightly on his feet. Any further delay and Kell saw that the chief would not be able to stand. What was happening was impossible, Kell's blood screamed.

The chief could not be felled by any mere wound.

Fuller swayed again and Kell knew that what was impossible was also true. And for the chief to die any way other than on his feet was intolerable.

"I will cover you," he found himself saying.

Fuller did not wait; he sprinted at the Klingons' position, emitting a battle cry that pierced the silence of the large facility.

Firing both phasers continuously, Fuller seemed to gain strength as he ran. He was twenty meters from the Klingons' position, then ten.

Then Kell saw a flash of uniform and the gleam of a Klingon disruptor. A large Klingon with a patch bolted over one eye appeared and Kell wanted to take a shot but he did not have a line of fire with Fuller in front of him.

Fuller took the shot and he did not miss. The Klingon was thrown back, mortally wounded.

Then another stepped out and Fuller was slammed by a full-power disruptor bolt at close range. There was a bright flash and Sam Fuller disappeared.

Kell felt the death wail rising in his throat and chest. He called out his pain and grief. He called out to the next world and told them to beware because a great warrior and a great man was coming.

When he was finished, he felt a calm settle over him and a resolve. Whoever had taken Fuller's life would soon take his last breath on this side of the River of Blood.

Kell's blood burned for revenge. It was not the human way, he knew, but it was his way, it was his people's way.

It was the Klingon way.

He checked his phaser to make sure it was set on full and prepared to finish this battle.

"Earther," he heard a voice say. "It is just you and I now."

There was something in the voice, something that cut through the rage, the heat of battle, and the call for vengeance that burned in his blood.

Something familiar.

"Earther," Karel said, using one of the few English words he knew. There was just one. The Earther was clever, but he had never faced a Klingon warrior before.

He had never tasted Klingon vengeance, but he would today.

Karel knew his opportunity for vengeance was slipping away. Once the *D'k tahg* left the system, the Klingon did not know when he might again make the Earthers pay for the crimes they had committed against his family and the Empire.

Now there was just one more Earther left in this complex. One last chance for his vengeance.

"Earther. It is just you and I now," Karel said, straining to remember the English words.

He waited a moment to let the Earther's fear work on him.

"Today you die," he said.

Karel stepped out from behind his position behind a large console. Then he stepped forward, his disruptor out.

Looking down, he took a brief second to adjust the weapon.

"Karel," a voice called out from the Earther's position.

For an instant, the sound of his name cut through the haze of his fury. Then he realized that his opponent was using some cowardly Earther trick. For that, Karel vowed to make the Earther die slowly.

"Brother, son of our father," the Earther said, and stepped into the open.

The invoking of Karel's father was the worst kind of cowardly Earther trick. Karel saw that the Earther had his weapons drawn.

...No, not drawn. The Earther's hands were reaching out for him.

Then Karel saw something in the Earther's eyes, something he recognized.

Too late. Driven by all the rage and grief in his blood, his traitor hand fired the disruptor, hitting the Earther... his brother... directly in the chest.

Kell felt time stop completely for a moment as he caught his brother's eyes. At first he thought Karel's voice was an illusion, a dream created by his fevered blood.

But when he saw his brother's eyes, he knew that Karel was real and was just a few meters in front of him.

He saw something else in Karel's eyes: recognition.

Then the disruptor came alive in Karel's hand and Kell felt the blast catch him in the chest and throw him back with great force.

He was amazed a moment later when he opened his eyes and saw the ceiling of the manufacturing plant.

"Kell!" a voice cut through the silence. He recognized the voice. It was the first Klingon voice to call his name since he put on this human's face. It was his brother's voice.

Kell smiled as he felt a great peace descend on him. His blood began to quiet, its roar to dim.

"Kell!" the voice called out, from above him now. The voice was full of pain. His brother was in pain.

Realizing his eyes were shut, Kell forced them open and saw something he thought he would never see again on this side of the River of Blood. Kell looked into his brother's eyes.

His brother was looking at him, his pain written on his face.

But Karel was not hurt, the pain was not for himself.

Taking his right hand, Kell reached for his chest. He felt the blood, the damage.

"It is all right," Kell said, glad to be speaking his native tongue. "You are here."

"How...how is this possible, Kell?" Karel said. "The Earthers...what did the Earthers do to you?"

Kell realized that his breath was not coming easily. By force of will, he made his chest move.

"Not the Earthers, my honored brother," Kell said. "I was sent by the High Command, but the choice was mine. I was sent to strike at the humans."

"The Earthers, we will defeat them. They will pay..." Karel said, his voice strained with pain.

"No," Kell said. "They have honor, there are many lies."

Kell felt darkness around him, closing in on him. Yet there was something he needed to do, something he could do for his brother and for his human friends. He had a duty. He had to make a report. Honor demanded truth.

Reaching into his uniform, Kell pulled out the round data tape and lifted it toward his brother. "Here, Karel. Take this."

Karel took it, uncomprehending.

"It contains truth," Kell said. "It is good to see you again, my brother."

Then Kell felt the darkness descend and his brother's face receded from his sight.

Klingons did not, *could not,* cry, because they lacked the tear ducts that humans had.

But they could wail.

Kell heard his brother wail now. Karel's death wail for his brother sounded through the space around them, seeming to shake the walls of the starbase. Because of his shame, his betrayal, and his dishonor, Kell knew the wail was wasted on him, yet its sound comforted him.

Kell hoped that if Kahless made a place for humans who lived, fought, and died with honor, then Benitez would be there. He found that that thought also comforted him.

He hoped that when he stood at the River of Blood he would catch a glimpse of his father and his human friend. Though he had no doubt that *Sto-Vo-Kor* would be denied him, he hoped that he would be granted that glimpse and a chance to call to them.

He had something he wanted say to them both....

Then he was beyond regret, beyond honor.

He heard the wail and its sound carried him.

Chapter Twenty-two

LESLIE PARRISH WOKE UP, her head swimming. She had to do something. There was something she had to do.

She tried to reach for her communicator and found her right arm would not obey her command.

Then she realized why: it was on fire.

Then memory slowly rose up in her mind. She had a phaser burn, which was why her arm no longer worked. But that was not important.

Ignoring the pain, she raised her left hand. There was something in it, a phaser. She tossed the weapon aside and reached behind her for her communicator.

She tried to flip it open.

A Starfleet security officer does not require assistance for such a simple task, a voice in her head said.

On the third try the device opened. By force of will

she found her voice and said, "Parrish to Anderson, come in Anderson.

"Parrish to Anderson, come in Anderson...

"Parrish to Anderson..."

She found herself fading...her eyes closing.

"Parrish to..."

Then she was aware of a sound. The turbolift doors were opening. Though she realized that it might be Klingons, she had to focus her energy on the simple task in front of her.

"Parrish...to...Anderson," she whispered.

"It's all right," a voice said from above her. It was human, she realized. "You are all right now."

"Parrish...to..."

Then a hand was removing the communicator from hers.

"It's all right. It's over now," the voice said.

"Parrish..." she whispered as darkness washed over her.

From his vantage point inside the small chamber, West could do little but look out at the ruined arboretum. The destruction was nearly total. Most of the smaller plants, the earth, and all of the equipment that was not attached to the floor had been sucked into space.

Even so, a few of the larger trees remained. And though they were no doubt dead or dying from lack of atmosphere, they looked serene and healthy as they presided over the destruction.

"We will have a lifetime to study our regrets," the admiral had once said to him.

Lieutenant West knew that would be very easy to do. He certainly had plenty of regrets. He had been a fool.

He had spent his time at Starfleet Academy mocking the legacy of men like Admiral Robert Justman, men like Captain Garth, men like his father.

They were men who had fought for a set of principles they believed in. Those principles had names—they were called the *United Federation of Planets* and *Starfleet Command.*

They had seen things and made sacrifices for those beliefs that West could have never imagined before, but now he could see all too well.

West had thought that he had known better than they had. He thought he could have avoided the fights that they had fought and won. He had questioned their motives, their means, and their ends.

Now he saw that there were some fights that came to you whether you sought them or not, whether you were ready or not.

And no matter how much you wished to understand other people, some of those people did not want to understand you. Sometimes they just wanted you to die.

All you could do then was to fight your best fight and make whatever sacrifices you needed to make.

And hope that was enough.

The admiral had known that. He had never had any doubts about what he was fighting for, and had not flinched when it came time to make his own sacrifice.

And his sacrifice had been enough. West had seen enough of the battle in space to know that. Admiral Justman had bought them time and a second chance to finish a battle that had begun twenty-five years ago when a young, untried lieutenant had done the impossible.

West would do everything he could to make certain that he helped to make the most of the chance the admiral had given them. He had a proposal for Admiral Solow on how to use understanding and a thorough knowledge of their history and culture to avoid conflict with other races. Failing that, the same knowledge could be used strategically to defeat them.

His work on the Klingons had begun, and he was certain that the fight was not over—and would not be over until the Federation defeated the Klingons absolutely and certainly. It was the only way to guarantee the future of the Federation and the principles it represented.

Thanks to the admiral, he had time to help with that task. And time for some other tasks as well.

When he returned to Earth, he would make two stops. The first would be to Admiral Solow to request a transfer to his strategic command. The second stop would be home.

He had no illusions that his father would be happy to see him. Yet they had to speak. West found that he had things he needed to say, things he needed his father to understand.

A simple apology would not do it, West knew. He knew his father and he knew he was in for a fight.

But West found that he was ready.

Suddenly a figure wearing an environmental suit appeared at the other side of the clear door.

A gloved hand rapped on the window and West stood

up. His rescuer made a motion that suggested opening a communicator.

The lieutenant checked for his and found that it was not there. Like many other things, it had been lost in the fighting.

He gestured with empty hands, and the head encased by the glass and silver suit nodded. A moment later, the rescuer produced a small transmitter and fixed it to the center of the door.

The rescuer gave West a thumbs-up and moved on.

Seconds later, Lieutenant West felt the transporter beam take him.

The door buzzed and Captain Kirk automatically checked the security monitor. Then he punched in a command code, and the large blast door near the entrance to auxiliary control opened.

"Mr. Spock, it's good to see you," Kirk said.

The Vulcan nodded. "You are well?"

"Yes," the captain replied. "Good work with the warp core."

"Thank you, sir, but much of the credit must go to Ensign Jawer," the Vulcan said.

Jawer had been involved in the System 1324 incident. He had turned a badly damaged Starfleet surplus shuttle into a formidable weapon against the Orions. The ensign had received a citation for his efforts. Perhaps another one was in order.

"Where is the ensign now?" he asked.

"Sickbay," the Vulcan said. "Dr. McCoy expects him to live."

Kirk was glad to hear that. "I look forward to reading your report, Mr. Spock," the captain said. Then he turned his attention to the four young starbase officers who had arrived with Spock.

To Kirk's surprise, he recognized them. They were the four officers who had been in the station control room during the siege.

"I'm glad to see you all made it," Kirk said, taking a step toward the science officer. "Lieutenant?"

"Akioshi, sir," she said.

"I presume you are here to relieve me," he said.

The young woman looked uncomfortable, and Kirk knew why. Technically he had been in command of the starbase for the last half hour or so.

"Ah...yes, sir," she said.

Kirk smiled, "I am pleased to transfer command to you. The station is yours, Lieutenant Akioshi."

She said, "Thank you, sir," but her face told a different story. She was not long out of the Academy and this was probably her first year in her first post. Now she was in command of a battle zone. She needed a boost. They all did.

"You all did very well today," Kirk said. "Thanks to your efforts and the efforts of this station's crew, the Klingons were stopped here and did not acquire a single dilithium crystal to fuel their war effort. And they have one Klingon cruiser which I expect will be some time in dry-dock somewhere. You gave the Klingons some surprises here today, quite a few of them. Besides the damage to their ship, the Klingons suffered heavy losses to their attack force due to strong resistance from station personnel."

That was true. Kirk had spent the last half hour coordinating search-and-rescue efforts and talking with survivors. Nearly half of the station's almost two-hundred-person crew had survived. And from what he could gather studying sensor logs and anecdotal data from the survivors, the Klingons' losses had been much heavier.

"The Klingons will no doubt think twice before taking on a Federation installation again. Well done," Kirk said.

Then he headed for the door. Spock immediately followed.

"Come on, Mr. Spock, let's go home."

Chapter Twenty-three

WHEN KIRK AND SPOCK stepped onto the bridge, the captain felt all eyes on them. He did not repress his smile and saw that he was not the only one smiling.

Mr. Scott got out of the command chair, beaming.

"Welcome back, sirs," Scotty said.

"Thank you, Mr. Scott," he said, taking a moment to scan the bridge. "And thanks to all of you who made sure that we had a ship to come back to. Excellent work today, all of you," he said.

Kirk settled into his command chair and felt some of the day's tension leaving him. He was home and the ship was safe. Whatever happened in the next few months, he took comfort in those two things.

The captain felt McCoy's absence on the bridge at times like this, but the doctor would be busy for some time with a full sickbay and his staff running back and forth to the starbase hospital, where more of the injured were being treated.

Given the size and scope of the conflict, there were relatively few wounded. The Klingons, apparently, did not believe in half measures. They did not take prisoners and they were not satisfied with merely injuring someone enough to keep them out of the fight.

And they were prepared to destroy a planet full of their own people, Kirk thought. Whatever happened, the Federation could not afford to lose to the Klingons.

He had a hundred duties to attend to and many of them were unpleasant. However, before he began there was something he needed to do. Looking around, he suspected the crew needed it just as much.

"Mr. Spock, how long until the Klingon escort arrives?" Kirk asked.

"Four point eight minutes," the Vulcan said.

"Lieutenant Uhura, hail the commander of the *D'k tahg*," Kirk said, gesturing to the damaged Klingon cruiser that was not at the center of the viewscreen.

"No response," Uhura said.

Kirk smiled. He had been expecting that.

"Mr. Sulu, please fire phasers across the Klingon ship's bow," he said. "And Sulu, make it *very* close."

"Aye, sir," Sulu said.

Kirk did not have to see the helmsman's face to know that he was smiling.

"Firing phasers," Sulu said as two red beams lanced out toward the Klingon ship and came remarkably close to the front of the vessel.

"Excellent shooting, Lieutenant," the captain said.

Kirk waited. It would not be long.

"I have the Klingon commander, Captain," Uhura said.

"Good," Kirk replied as he stood up. "Put him on the screen and put the transmission on shipwide audio."

A moment later a Klingon appeared on the screen. The Klingon's face was unreadable.

"I am Captain James T. Kirk of the *Starship Enterprise*," Kirk said.

"I am Koloth, captain of the Klingon battle cruiser *D'k tahg*. I protest your resumption of hostilities when a cease-fire agreement has been agreed to by both our governments."

"That was not hostility, Captain Koloth, I assure you," Kirk said. "If hostility had been our intention, we would not have missed and you would not still be there talking to me."

There it was: rage. The Klingon was not so hard to read after all.

"Consider it a message," Kirk continued. "And I have another message for you to take back to your High Command. We know what you were doing here today, Captain. And we know what the Klingon Empire is planning. You were beaten by a starship and her crew. You were defeated by the *lesser* race you call Earthers. There are eleven more out there waiting for any Klingon vessel or force to move against the Federation. If you choose to forget the lesson of today, we will be glad to reenlighten you.

"We are a peaceful people, by nature, but when we are roused to fighting we do not lose. The Klingon Empire will challenge us at its own peril," Kirk said.

Kirk was not sure how the Klingon commander

would respond, but he had not expected the smile that suddenly graced Koloth's lips.

"My dear Captain Kirk, I have found our encounter today exhilarating. I look forward to meeting you again."

The Klingon's face disappeared from the screen and was replaced by the Klingon cruiser.

"Captain," Uhura said. "We're being hailed from the second Klingon cruiser."

"Keep them waiting for a few minutes, Lieutenant," Kirk said. "Then talk to them and see that they take the *D'k tahg* and get out of Federation space as quickly as possible."

"Yes, sir," she said.

From what Kirk knew about the Klingons, the commander would see it as an insult that Kirk did not speak to him personally.

Good.

"Captain," Uhura said. "I also have the prime minister of the government on the planet's surface."

"On screen, Lieutenant," Kirk said, and a moment later a surprisingly young man who was in his early thirties and was wearing civilian clothes appeared on the screen.

Kirk smiled and said, "This is Captain James T. Kirk of the *Starship Enterprise*. What can I do for you, Mr. Prime Minister?"

As soon as the prime minister began speaking, his face twisted in a way that told Kirk everything he needed to know. "This is Prime Minister Althaus. I would like to know exactly when Starfleet intends to continue their pullout. We have negotiated a very clear schedule, Captain."

"With all due respect, Mr. Prime Minister, there is a new security concern that—"

"We have an arrangement!" Althaus said.

Kirk stood up and raised his own voice. "Mr. Althaus, a fully armed Klingon battle cruiser, a *second* Klingon battle cruiser, is approaching this system and will be here in a few minutes, but if you like the *Enterprise* will leave the system right now."

"I...did not mean...just the *Enterprise*," Althaus said. Then the prime minister was momentarily silent. When he spoke again, it was with a much softer voice. "We want to be reasonable, Captain, but we have an arrangement with Starfleet and a timetable."

"I am afraid that that timetable will have to change. Like it or not, your planet has just become very important both because of its strategic position and its dilithium crystals. And the Klingons know you are there," Kirk said.

The prime minister was once again speechless.

"Now, we will have to finish this discussion tomorrow," the captain said. "We have lost a lot of people today and we're very busy. Kirk out."

The captain waited until the Klingon ship arrived, engaged its tractor beam on the *D'k tahg,* and warped out of the system.

When the two ships were well on their way to Klingon space, Kirk got to his feet and said, "Mr. Spock, the bridge is yours. I will be in my quarters."

When his doors closed behind him, Kirk sat at his desk, hit the intercom, and said, "Kirk to sickbay."

There was a pause of a few seconds, and then the doctor's voice replied, "McCoy here."

"Bones, what is your situation?" Kirk said.

He could hear the doctor take a breath before he spoke. "We have everyone stabilized and the last one just came out of surgery."

"Do we have a count of the casualties?" Kirk asked.

"Not yet, but it's bad, Jim, maybe the worst this ship has seen. We're setting up morgues on the station and on board. It will be a while before we have a final count, because there were some disintegrations. We do have some positive identifications and, well, Jim, we have confirmed that both Sam Fuller and Admiral Justman are dead."

Kirk was silent for a long moment.

"We will have a full report by midday tomorrow," McCoy said finally.

"Thank you, Bones, Kirk out," the captain said as he hit the intercom button that closed the communication.

It seemed impossible. Admiral Justman was the Hero of Donatu V. A legend and part of Starfleet's living history.

Of course, Kirk had studied the battle at the Academy. And he had done some further research and had read the admiral's reports of the time.

The then-lieutenant's account in his own words had had a powerful effect on Kirk as a cadet. They had also helped shape the next twenty-five years of Starfleet history.

What had Justman called the *Constitution...?*

A ship of dreams.

The performance of that ship, unfinished and untested, had helped insure the future of the starship program.

Now there were twelve ships...twelve dreams.

And those twelve might be the only things that stood in the way of the end of Starfleet, the end of the Federation: the end of everything.

The admiral had left something behind. He had inspired countless other cadets and he had achieved much in his more than quarter-century career.

That should have comforted Kirk, but it did not. They had all lost something precious that could not be reclaimed.

And Sam. He had come to believe that the chief was indestructible, like his father. Michael Fuller had also survived the Battle of Donatu V. Kirk had meant to introduce Justman to Michael's son Sam and to ask the admiral if he and the elder Fuller had known each other in the battle.

That was when Kirk thought there was still time for such things.

The captain had seen Sam Fuller work miracles. He and his people had saved the settlement in 1324. Against impossible odds, Sam and the others had saved nearly all of them.

In the entire time Kirk had known Sam, the man had never doubted himself, had never wavered. He had known his duty and had done it without hesitation.

The captain was sure that that was how he had died.

Now Kirk would have to tell his father, Michael Fuller, who had saved Kirk's own life when he was a young, overeager, overconfident lieutenant serving on the *Farragut*.

Kirk would have to tell Michael Fuller that he had not been able to do the same for his son.

* * *

Lieutenant West was exhausted. He knew he needed to sleep, but found that he could not and did not want to. When he closed his eyes, he found that images he did not want to see came unbidden.

The crew of the *Enterprise* had taken pains to make him comfortable. He had been given comfortable quarters to himself, yet a different room than the one he had when he had arrived on board with the admiral.

He wondered if someone was trying to spare his feelings by changing the rooms. He appreciated the effort, but knew that whatever demons he had now would follow him much farther than a deck or two on this starship.

West knew he could not silence those demons while he did nothing but wait. Now he saw that the images he saw when he closed his eyes and the sounds he heard in the silence around him were not demons at all—they were a warning.

A warning that he could heed.

West got up from the bed and sat at the small desk. One of the crew had moved his personal things from his old quarters to the new one. It was the kind of thing that Admiral Justman might have arranged, except that West knew, of course, that that was impossible.

Reaching for his data tapes, he chose the one he needed and placed it into the computer. If it was later and less busy on the starship, he would have used the central computer, but the terminal in front of him would be fine for now.

He had added to the Klingon cultural and historical database that he had compiled at Starfleet Command, augmenting it with data he had found elsewhere and most recently in the *Enterprise*'s own computer.

As a result he had much of what he needed in front of him.

West knew that many in Starfleet Command still thought the Klingons were invincible, yet West knew that was not true.

He had seen the *Enterprise* and the crew on board the starbase turn what should have been a crushing blow against the Federation into a sound defeat for the Klingons.

A defeat.

Something the Klingons would never have expected, but something they understood. As a warrior culture, they lived for victory, but they did understand defeat.

West knew that in the 1324 and 7348 incidents the Klingons had suffered setbacks, but they had been using Orions as intermediaries.

This time, the Klingons had put themselves into the fight and they had been soundly beaten, achieving none of their objectives. Instead, they had lost many warriors and had nearly lost a ship.

Defeat was the key. Not in a limited battle, or in a single incident, but in an all-out and decisive battle with Starfleet.

Only then could the Federation make a lasting peace with the Klingon Empire. Only then would the Federation have real security and an opportunity to fulfill its dreams and Starfleet its mission.

Lieutenant West got back to work.

* * *

Karel's blood no longer burned. It now ran cold in his veins.

In the transporter room Koloth had met him and said, "You are the last, you were ordered back an hour ago. You are a good warrior, Karel, but never let me doubt that you will follow my orders immediately and without question."

Karel had nodded and said, "Yes, sir."

"You were nearly left behind with the Earthers," Koloth said.

Karel had considered that. He had considered simply staying where he was with his brother's body in his arms until the Earthers came and captured him.

Capture was unthinkable, but no less unthinkable than what his own hand had done.

He had once thought that it was impossible for the cowardly and weak Earthers to have killed his brother. Kell, whose spirit and courage was too great to be felled by mere Earthers. Kell, who had once, as a young and small boy, brought down a large charging *targ* by himself while older and more experienced hunters ran for their lives.

Karel had been right. Earthers had not, could not kill his brother; only he and his burning Klingon blood had been able to do that.

And now that blood, which had burned with the glory of battle, ran cold with his shame.

He knew he deserved no better than to suffer and die in the care of Earther interrogators. He certainly did not deserve to see Qo'noS again.

Yet to avoid his fate through inaction and to let the Earthers take his life would shame him further. He might not have his brother's courage, but facing the consequences of what he had done was the least that he could do to honor his brother's memory.

And he had questions about why his brother was wearing an Earther's face and why Karel was told by Klingon command that his brother had been killed by Earthers in a cowardly attack.

So many lies and deceptions. Lies that had pitted Klingon warriors of the same blood, *of the same father*, against each other.

He would have his answers, answers that lay in a small bloodstained data disk in his hand.

"Did you strike the Earthers additional blows?" Koloth asked.

"No," Karel said. "I accomplished nothing." *Except the death of my father's son,* he thought.

Koloth studied him. What the captain might be seeing in his face, Karel could not even guess. For a moment, Karel considered telling Koloth some of what he had learned. The captain was a Klingon of honor and a follower of Kahless.

He had believed that Koloth might be a great ally to him. Karel decided that he might test the limits of Koloth's honor, but he would not do it until he knew more.

After a moment, Koloth said, "You are dismissed."

Gripping the disk firmly, Karel headed for his quarters.

Chapter Twenty-four

LESLIE PARRISH WOKE and instantly recognized that she was in sickbay. She had a moment of peaceful clarity before the truth came crashing down on her.

Jon was dead. He had gotten her to safety and now he was dead.

She remembered security officers coming to get her. The fact that there had been anyone to find her told her that they had won.

Jon had not fought for nothing. He had not died for nothing.

Yet those thoughts gave her no comfort.

She wondered about the others. Had they all died too? Most likely.

She turned her head to scan the room. Next to her she saw someone lying on the bed. Someone she did recognize.

It was Ensign Jawer. He looked unconscious, but he was alive.

She lay there for a long time before she heard footsteps approaching. Turning her head, she saw the captain approaching with Dr. McCoy.

She tried to push herself to a sitting position. To her mild surprise, she found that her right arm worked. Yet to put it to any use caused a nearly blinding flash of pain there.

A gentle but firm hand on her shoulder told her to stop trying. It was the doctor.

"Stay still for now, Ensign," Dr. McCoy said. "Your arm will be fine, but give it a chance to heal."

Then he turned to Kirk and said, "Just a few minutes, Captain."

"Understood, Doctor," Kirk said as McCoy walked away.

"Ensign Parrish, how are you feeling?" the captain said, a look of genuine concern on his face.

That look, that concern, threatened her composure most of all. She forced her emotions back down and said, "Ensign Jawer and I are the only survivors of the squad?"

"Yes, I'm sorry, Ensign. Chief Fuller and Ensign Anderson were lost in the fighting."

Parrish nodded. She had known that, felt it.

"I'm sorry for your loss, Ms. Parrish," Kirk said.

"Thank you, Captain," she said. Then she said nothing. She found that she did not trust her voice.

"I understand that you and Jon Anderson were close," Kirk said.

Parrish could only nod. *Yes, we were* close.

"All of his personal effects, medals, and citations are being returned to his family on Earth. However..." Kirk held up a small container. "However, I have his equipment. His phaser, his communicator, and his tricorder. They are yours if you would like them."

Parrish managed a grim smile and even a few words. "Thank you, Captain."

"Well then," Kirk said, straightening himself. "I will be back to see you later."

Then, with a nod, the captain turned and left.

Parrish managed to keep her composure until she heard the door close behind him.

She remembered Jon's last words to her, "I promise." He had promised to return to her. She had seen something in his eyes then, however. He had wanted to return, she was sure. Just as she was sure that he had known then it would be impossible.

He was gone.

Then it came, the flood, the avalanche.

She did not fight it. She felt it, his loss, his absence. She felt *him*.

Kirk knew that the casualty report would be the most difficult part of the briefing, and he was right.

At the moment, Spock spoke to the assembled group of department heads sitting around the briefing-room table. All except McCoy, who was tending to the injured and had logged many trips on the transporter going back and forth from the ship to the station.

"Due to the number of disintegrations, we had to use headcounts of surviving *Enterprise* and starbase personnel as well as eyewitness accounts to reach the total," he said.

One hundred and thirty-seven people, Kirk thought. Twenty-four of them members of his own crew.

He had lost two security section chiefs and had nearly lost Giotto, according to reports of the skirmish with Klingon troops on the surface.

The number was higher if they counted the total lost since 1324, where thirteen of the twenty-one-person team was lost.

And of those eight survivors only two were still alive after yesterday. It had been close with Ensign Jawer but he would live. And Ensign Parrish would be back on her feet in days.

Replacement crew was on its way.

Kirk rejected the thought. You replaced equipment. You even replaced vessels that were lost. You did not replace people.

"Captain?" Spock said.

"Yes?" Kirk said, shaking himself out of his reverie. Kirk looked around the table; the others were looking to him.

"Status of station and ship, Mr. Scott," Kirk said.

"The new dilithium reaction chamber is on its way, Captain," Scotty said. "All other repairs on the *Enterprise* are progressing. The real challenge is going to be rebuilding the station. Not only were there large areas of destruction, but there was a lot of damage done to the station's own manufacturing plant. Replacement components are on the way, but we have a big job ahead of us. However, we also have more volunteers from the crew than we know what to do with. There will be no shortage of people for the job."

The captain was not surprised, but he was pleased. Rebuilding would be good for the crew right now. They had seen enough destruction in the last few weeks. It would help them to be part of some creation.

"Of course," Mr. Scott said, "it would help to have access to some of the resources on the surface, but we have had trouble securing...full cooperation."

"I will be addressing that and a number of other issues with the prime minister and planetary senate later today," Kirk said. "Thank you, you are dismissed."

As the group began to file out, the intercom beeped.

"Kirk here," he said.

"I have Commodore Decker for you, sir."

"I'll take it in here." When Decker's face appeared on the small screen, Kirk said, "Matt, you're well."

Decker nodded. "How about you, Jim."

"We're all better now that you and the *Constellation* are here, Matt," Kirk said.

"Glad to help. I only wish we could have been here sooner. I'm sorry for your crew, Captain," Decker said.

Kirk nodded.

"Our orders are to stay until the job is done, so whatever you need, Jim," Decker said.

"Thank you, Matt. Actually, there is something you can help me with immediately. I have a meeting later today with the planetary authorities. I could use some backup."

Decker smiled. "I am at your disposal, Captain. I will see you shortly. Decker out."

When the screen went dark, Kirk hit the controls to

show the *Constellation* as it approached. The captain imagined a young Lieutenant Justman seeing that sight for the first time as the *U.S.S. Constitution* arrived to help at the Battle of Donatu V.

Then Kirk did not have to imagine how Justman felt. He knew.

It was a ship of dreams.

A moment later the intercom beeped again.

"Captain, this is McCoy. I'm in sickbay and I think you'd better come down here."

"On my way, Bones," Kirk said as he got up and headed for the door.

In sickbay, Kirk found the doctor and Mr. Spock in McCoy's office looking at the viewscreen on his desk.

"Remarkable," Spock said.

"What is it, Bones?" Kirk said.

McCoy looked up and said, "It's the post-mortem report on Ensign Anderson. There were some irregularities."

"Irregularities?" Kirk asked.

"Dr. M'Benga performed the actual post-mortem and noticed some significant anatomical...differences. The genetic test proved what he suspected." McCoy pointed at the image on the viewscreen. Kirk recognized the double helix of DNA.

"Proved what?" Kirk said.

"Jim, that man was a Klingon," McCoy said.

"A...what? That's impossible," Kirk said.

"We ran and reran the tests, Captain. Ensign Jon Anderson was a Klingon. He was surgically altered to look like a human. Even his bone marrow was altered, with gene therapy that allowed it to make blood that still had the properties of Klingon blood but had a more or less human red color," the doctor said.

"Captain," Spock said, "Admiral Justman did refer to operatives working for the Klingons in Starfleet. We had been working under the assumption that those assassins and saboteurs were humans in the employ of the Klingon Empire. Now we have evidence that they were Klingons surgically altered to appear as humans."

"But Anderson has a family. I've spoken to his mother," Kirk said.

"Jim," McCoy said, "I have no doubt that Jon Anderson was a real person who entered Starfleet training. I checked his medical records and found his last physical. He was human, all right."

"Most likely," Spock added, "the real Jon Anderson was abducted by the Klingon Empire and replaced with a Klingon surgically altered to look like him."

"Then the real Jon Anderson..." Kirk said.

"Is certainly dead," Spock said.

Kirk could not believe it. He had sat with Jon Anderson, had reviewed Sam Fuller's reports about what the young man had done in the 1324 incident. Kirk had given Anderson the medals and citations himself.

And according to survivors' reports, including reports from Ensign Parrish, he had fought very hard against the Klingons on the starbase.

"I know it doesn't make any sense, Jim," McCoy said, sensing Kirk's own thoughts. "I spoke to him myself right after the 7348 mission. And I'm not sure he was working for the Klingons in the end."

"Why?" Kirk said.

"A feeling, Captain," McCoy said. "When I talked to him he was nearly sick with grief over the losses in the mine. I can't give you proof, but I don't think he was faking any of it. Plus, it is a harsh mission for the Empire to send anyone on. It's a one-way ticket."

"How so?" Kirk asked.

"The Klingon agent's cover would be blown the first time he had to receive treatment in sickbay," McCoy said, "or go for a routine physical. No one, least of all the Klingons, expected them to live long."

"Captain," Spock said. "There is the possibility that Anderson had assistance of others to maintain his ruse. He was close to Ensign Parrish—"

"No," Kirk said definitively. He had just met with her and had just looked into her eyes. She was nearly drowning in her grief, but she was no Klingon collaborator. "It wouldn't make any sense," he said. "Klingon agents would need to operate in complete secrecy to limit their chance of exposure."

McCoy nodded. "Will you tell her the truth?"

Kirk shook his head. "No. Even we don't know the truth here."

"What about the young man's parents?" McCoy said.

Kirk had not considered that. He thought about it and shook his head again. "Tell them that their son was captured by the Empire and most likely died at the hands of a very skilled Klingon interrogator? No. I will tell them that their son was a highly decorated officer in Starfleet who died in the performance of his duty."

"That would seem to be a kindness," Spock said.

"We do, however," Kirk said, "have to make an immediate report to Starfleet Command. By this time to-morrow we can have all the Klingon agents in Starfleet in custody. Perhaps if we put a stop to their hidden weapons and close the security breaches they caused, the Klingon Empire will think even harder about taking on the Federation."

"I have already put together a simple scanning program Fleet doctors can use to detect them," McCoy said.

That is something else that will come from this mission, Kirk thought. They would likely never know the truth about the intentions of the Klingon who wore the face of Ensign Jon Anderson, but the truth of his biology would now help the Federation against the Empire.

"After today, no Klingon agent will be able to infiltrate Starfleet again," Kirk said. Yes, it was something.

Epilogue

KIRK WAITED FOR A MOMENT outside the door, listening.

From inside the transporter room he heard the chief say, "There are no old Starfleet security officers," and the laughter that followed.

He smiled himself. That had been Sam Fuller's joke. And before that it had been his father's.

Usually Kirk waited until the chief was done swearing them in to make his appearance.

Not today.

Kirk stepped through the doors as the chief was finishing the address. Then he heard what he came early to hear.

"Repeat after me," the chief said. " 'I solemnly swear to uphold the regulations of Starfleet Command as well as the laws of the United Federation of Planets, to become ambassadors of peace and goodwill, to represent the highest ideals of peace and brotherhood, to protect and serve the Federation and its member worlds, to serve the interests of peace, to respect the Prime Directive, and to offer aid to any and all beings that request it.' "

Phrase by phrase the new officers repeated the oath. As they did, Kirk noted how impossibly *young* they all looked. Yet they were eager to begin their service, eager to be a part of the crew of a starship, on the *Enterprise.*

Well, Kirk knew how they felt.

"Captain," the chief said, then turned to the assembled group and said, "Recruits, I present Captain James T. Kirk."

Kirk stepped forward and said, "Welcome to the *Enterprise.* I look forward to getting to know each of you in turn. For now, I'll trust you to Lieutenant Parrish's capable hands."

"Thank you, Captain," Leslie Parrish said.

"Thank *you,* Chief," Kirk said as he left the transporter room.

Karel had waited weeks for this moment. He had haggled with the trader for appearance's sake, but he would have paid much more for what he now held in his hand.

His next stop was the rooming house. Again, he haggled on the price of the room so he would not arouse suspicion.

Entering the small room, he noted that it was sparely furnished, with only a bed and a small table—the people who used it had need of nothing else.

Yet it was more than sufficient for Karel's purposes. All he needed was some time away from the Empire's surveillance cameras.

Here, at liberty on a planet with nothing but illegal trade to recommend it, Karel had found what he needed.

The Klingon took the data disk from his pocket and put it into the recently acquired Starfleet tricorder. There was equipment on the *D'k tahg* that he could have used to examine the contents of the disk, but there would have been too many eyes on him, and too many eyes would learn what he was about to learn.

While Karel trusted his captain, Koloth, he was not ready to share this with even him yet.

The device was simple to use, and Karel quickly found a file with his name on it. He hit a button and he heard his brother Kell's voice.

"My honored brother Karel. It is your brother Kell. When I began this mission, I had believed that I might succeed and see you once again. I now know that that will never happen. I suspect it was never meant to . . ."

Karel listened to the recording in silence until his brother's voice concluded with, "I regret, my brother, that I will not see you again, or our honored mother, but I carry your faces with me for the rest of my time in this world and I will take them to the next. Your brother, Kell."

Karel did not move for a long time after the recording was finished.

His brother had served the Empire so bravely, sacrificed so much. Yet the High Command had used his honor and his loyalty to strip him of his face and send him on a mission built on lies, to help defeat a foe that the Empire could not defeat in open battle, to help defeat a foe that should not be an enemy at all.

Lies.

Kahless has spoken of truth as a road to honor. Where was the honor in the Empire now? Where was the honor in destroying a whole planet of Klingon brothers to kill humans?

Where was the honor in wasting a spirit such as his brother Kell's?

Karel knew the answer. There was much dishonor in the Empire now. He had known it, had sensed it for some time. Yet he had chosen to remain blind to what his younger brother hand seen so clearly. His brother had had the courage to see that which Karel himself could not face.

But now that Karel saw, he would not close his eyes again.

There was but one path to honor. Kahless had taught them that. He would take that path and would honor his brother by ridding the Empire of its secrets and its lies, by ridding it of its dishonor, by seeing that the Empire that Kahless had begun did not waste its spirit and its blood on pointless conflict.

He would never be the Klingon that his brother was, but he would do what he could.

From this point forward, he pledged that his family would do nothing less. There was still much that was true within the Empire. The Gorkon family would help the Klingon Empire find its honor and defend it as Kahless once defended his people against the tyrant Molor.

Honor demanded nothing less.

About the Author

Kevin Ryan is the author of two novels and the co-author of two more. He has written a bunch of comic books and has also written for television. He lives in New York with his wife and four children. He can be reached at Kryan1964@aol.com.

Look for STAR TREK fiction from Pocket Books

Star Trek®

Star Trek®: The Original Series

Star Trek: The Next Generation®

Star Trek: Deep Space Nine®

Star Trek: Voyager®

Star Trek®: Day of Honor

#1 • *Ancient Blood* • Diane Carey
#2 • *Armageddon Sky* • L.A. Graf
#3 • *Her Klingon Soul* • Michael Jan Friedman
#4 • *Treaty's Law* • Dean Wesley Smith & Kristine Kathryn Rusch
The Television Episode • Michael Jan Friedman
Day of Honor Omnibus • various

Star Trek®: The Captain's Table

#1 • *War Dragons* • L.A. Graf
#2 • *Dujonian's Hoard* • Michael Jan Friedman
#3 • *The Mist* • Dean Wesley Smith & Kristine Kathryn Rusch
#4 • *Fire Ship* • Diane Carey
#5 • *Once Burned* • Peter David
#6 • *Where Sea Meets Sky* • Jerry Oltion
The Captain's Table Omnibus • various

Star Trek®: The Dominion War

#1 • *Behind Enemy Lines* • John Vornholt
#2 • *Call to Arms...* • Diane Carey
#3 • *Tunnel Through the Stars* • John Vornholt
#4 • *...Sacrifice of Angels* • Diane Carey

Star Trek®: Section 31™

Rogue • Andy Mangels & Michael A. Martin
Shadow • Dean Wesley Smith & Kristine Kathryn Rusch
Cloak • S.D. Perry
Abyss • Dean Weddle & Jeffrey Lang

Star Trek®: Gateways

#1 • *One Small Step* • Susan Wright
#2 • *Chainmail* • Diane Carey
#3 • *Doors Into Chaos* • Robert Greenberger
#4 • *Demons of Air and Darkness* • Keith R.A. DeCandido
#5 • *No Man's Land* • Christie Golden
#6 • *Cold Wars* • Peter David
#7 • *What Lay Beyond* • various
Epilogue: Here There Be Monsters • Keith R.A. DeCandido

Star Trek®: The Badlands

#1 • Susan Wright
#2 • Susan Wright

Star Trek®: Dark Passions

#1 • Susan Wright
#2 • Susan Wright

Star Trek® Omnibus Editions

Invasion! Omnibus • various
Day of Honor Omnibus • various
The Captain's Table Omnibus • various
Star Trek: Odyssey • William Shatner with Judith and Garfield Reeves-Stevens
Millennium Omnibus • Judith and Garfield Reeves-Stevens
Starfleet: Year One • Michael Jan Friedman

Other Star Trek® Fiction

Legends of the Ferengi • Ira Steven Behr & Robert Hewitt Wolfe
Strange New Worlds, vol. I, II, III, IV, and V • Dean Wesley Smith, ed.
Adventures in Time and Space • Mary P. Taylor, ed.
Captain Proton: Defender of the Earth • D.W. "Prof" Smith
New Worlds, New Civilizations • Michael Jan Friedman
The Lives of Dax • Marco Palmieri, ed.
The Klingon Hamlet • Wil'yam Shex'pir
Enterprise Logs • Carol Greenburg, ed.
Amazing Stories Anthology • various